ZIMERA
A Novel

By
Kareen Lopez Samuels

Cadmus Publishing
www.CadmusPublishing.com

© 2020 Kareen Lopez Samuels
Cover art by Sonia Trivedi-Bindra

Published by Cadmus Publishing
www.cadmuspublishing.com

ISBN: 978-1-7343644-8-4

All rights reserved. Copyright under Berne Copyright Convention, Universal Copyright Convention, and Pan-American Copyright Convention. No part of this book may be reproduced, stored in a retrieval system, or transmitted in any form, or by any means, electronic, mechanical, photocopying, recording or otherwise, without prior permission of the author.

This is a work of fiction; therefore names, characters, places, and incidents are the products of the author's imagination or are used fictitiously. Any resemblance to actual events, locales, or persons, living or dead, is entirely coincidental.

Dedication

This book is dedicated to my mom (deceased), dad, husband, my two girls, all my brothers, Ann Marie Steele Daley (my sister and friend); all my relatives and friends, for all their love. I consider myself blessed beyond measure to have each and everyone of you in my life.

My greatest desire is that this book brings healing to those who dare to flip through her pages; that you will come away with the most fitting and appropriate lessons for your specific situation.

"But there was no need
to be ashamed of tears,
for tears bore witness
that a man had
the greatest of courage,
the courage to suffer."
Viktor E. Frankl

To everything there is a season, and a time to every
purpose
under the heaven:
A time to be born, and a time to die; a time to plant,
and
a time to pluck up that which is planted;
A time to kill, and a time to heal; a time to break
down, and a time to build up;
A time to weep, and a time to laugh; a time to
mourn, and a time to dance;
A time to cast away stones, and a time to gather
stones together; a little to embrace,
and a time to refrain from embracing;
A time to get and a time to lose; a time to keep, and a
to cast away;
A time to rend, and a time to sew; a time to keep
silence, and a time to speak;
A time to love and a time to hate; a time of war, and
a time of peace.
(Eccl. 3.1-8 NKJ)

Table of Contents

Prologue 1
Cyril's Nightmare 4
Cyril's Secret 9
Austin's Assessment 15
Aunt Felecie 18
A Time to Die 25
The Fallout 29
The Funeral 38
Unstated Truths 42
Cyril's Burden 50
Cyril's Anguish – The Aftermath 59
A Time to Mourn 62
Cyril meets Zimera 67
Austin's Torment 73
Cyril's Time to Heal 79
A Time to Pluck up That which has been Planted .. 89
Zimera: A Time to live 93
The Fight 96
My Dinner Party 102
Austin's Resolve 112
Cyril's Dilemma 116
Austin's Transformation 119

Cyril's Crisis	122
The Big Reveal	125
Fiona's Relief	132
Cyril's Miracle	138
Cyril's Show	146
Epilogue	149
Acknowledgements	151
About the Author	154

Prologue

I am Zimera. I live in an in between realm: between the quick and the dead, between the weak and the strong, between love and hate, between generations of families and the spirits that oppress them. I am an ancestral spirit and I foster healing in families. I am by no means a deity of any kind but I have lived from the first man, Adam, fell. I come through different channels: through varying bloodlines and I come for many and various reasons. I am able to take on any form that suits the situation. By and large, I don't normally know what form I'm going to take until it happens. Also, as a general rule, I cross over to the world of the living in times of crisis, when a loved one in real time needs help – when he or she is in danger of losing his soul. *For what doth it profit a man to gain this whole world and lose his one soul.*

I always give of my best but with humans it's hard to tell. Humans are sentient beings. This means, they are created to act on their own freewill and volition so there is an edict against forcing them to conform against their will. Ever so often, I fail dismally because the *Cupitus* (the beloved one) or my assignment, might not be in a place where he or she is ready to accept the help I offer. This gives credence to the fact that, I do try, but the specific service I offer is not for everyone.

Also, I never know where I will be dispatched next. I don't make up the schedule. I sometimes make several appearances among the same family members. I am tuned into various sound waves, channels that transmit deep groaning in the spirit world, a voice so anguished, so deeply pained that it breaks all the barriers, all the unbelief in their bloodline and captivates my attention or that of another ancestral being. When the pain is this great it becomes imperative to break through generational strongholds. At times, I have to fight through generational spirits of apathy or lethargy and the uncanny ability to self destruct. The *Cupitus* is often so shackled that he fails to see the need for release. It's almost a situation where an animal has been caged for so long, and has gotten accustomed to being bound that even if you open the cage, they will not advance their escape. Obviously, the *Cupitus* doesn't get to this place overnight. Hence, he fails to perceive that he is in bondage. This bondage can be a wall of protection built around the self to protect both the Id and Ego. In cases like this, offering freedom is never easy.

Invariably, in so doing, this ultimately leads to a destruction of the will to live; the will to fight. Humans grow in leaps and bounds; life is made up of happy moments, sad moments and sometimes moments that involve them fighting for survival in a harsh world. No matter who the human is, he or she is sometimes entrenched in a struggle, that's just the way life is. Some humans lose their ability to empathize because they are overly sensitive souls so to alleviate pain they stop caring; while others, have found a way to go numb, to resist pain. Hence, losing their ability to empathize with others. Still others, known as empaths are so connected to human emotions that they absorb other people's *umzabalazo* (struggle).

  I am not a human; therefore, none of these rules apply. Not withstanding, I have come to understand humans and their emotions but I am in no way shackled by their fervor. I am not constrained by emotions either. That being said, in my human form I am able to intuitively mirror and reject emotions.

Chapter 1

Cyril's Nightmare

It always starts this way, a dream about shadows – being lost in the shadows. And in the tradition of dreams, quickly escalates into utter darkness. Darkness that's so thick that you can almost touch it. As a matter of fact, that's the natural inclination to reach out and touch it; to hold it up to your face. Eventually, you do get use to the darkness especially after having this dream a few times. Ultimately, the free fall is frightening and you scream as loudly as you can but then you realize that you are all alone and just like in waking moments, no one, absolutely no one is coming to help, no one is coming to your rescue. That's singularly one of the most petrifying thoughts that can afflict a human being, the deep sense of isolation which leads to alienation.

At first, I just let it happen – the free fall I mean– which is both exhilarating and terrifying at the same time. Then, as falling becomes more familiar, I learn to play with the shadows, imagine faces and indiscreet objects as they pass me by.

On this particular night – that too – it is always at night. Why is it always at night? The free fall intensifies and for some other worldly reason, I can some how sense that the ultimate purpose will be different tonight. A sense of deeper darkness and a falling away of everything I know to be true; to be real, to be inveterate. Naturally, I fight as at other times, to rouse myself, to put a halt to the free fall. Soon, it becomes obvious that all my old tricks are outdated: I am unable to sway my course and resistance is futile.

After struggling for a while, against everything that is rational and wholesome, I decide to go with it to see what happens. Again, I rely on the ordinary, to wake up before I hit rock bottom. Fortunately, this does not happen as I have an appointment with destiny, against my best judgment and natural proclivities. I brace myself for the inevitable splatter of my innards. Luckily, this doesn't happen but the shadows and strange sounds loom in the distance, becoming bigger and louder. I attempt to cover my eyes and ears but there is just no escaping the onslaught; as that is both useless and difficult to accomplish in flight.

That's when I hear the word – mind you, in all my midnight rendezvous – there has always been words - from which I could discern implicit meanings, even when spoken in a foreign language. The resounding word of the night is ZIMERA. The peculiarity of the word is not in the word itself but how it is expressed – almost like an incantation – an omen. After this pronouncement, I am unable to process what I've heard, because the shadows materialize into unexpected images.

Previously, I just imagined their existence but it seems like all my dark imaginings have called them into sharp focus. Strange being a relative concept in my current situation, I mean images that I have seen before or in some way know of their existence, but chose to forget, appear with an added dimension of gruesomeness. For instance, there is that bat with red, translucent wings and talons, it turns into a cobra that wraps itself around me, an eagle suddenly makes an appearance, quickly swallowing the snake and they both disappear. A dead boy wrapped in yellow florescent light with wine, red blood dripping from a huge gash in his abdomen. I quickly turn away because I do not want to witness his organs spilling or capture his face. Most images are easily forgotten but for me, not faces.

Over the din of the moment, I hear a guttural sound and I wonder where it comes from soon, I discover the source of the disruption - it is me – I am the guttural sound. Based on the dryness and soreness of my throat I realize that I am making the sound. Suddenly, I feel myself being shaken unceremoniously and I check to see if it is the boy; thankfully, it isn't because I am awake. I am awake! Joyfully and jubilantly awake in my own bed, in my own room, in my own house not in some dungeon; soaking in perspiration, being embraced by my life long friend.

"Cyril, Cyril, Cyril! Wake up!" "Are you ok?" "Speak to me man!"

My friend, Austin came to dinner earlier and decided to sleep over! I forgot that I wasn't alone — not tonight. Usually, I am alone but Austin decided to sleep over. It was just like old times when we were growing up.

"I'm good, I'm good!" I manage to stutter, tasting the rawness of my throat, fighting back bile and feeling the start of a migraine. He simultaneously strokes and hugs me as if I'm his child; despite my three years difference in age.

I catch my breath and recover my voice. "Can you please get me some water?"

Almost immediately, I hear the tap in the bathroom running and Austin is by my side again.

"What was that screaming about man? It sounded like.... like screams from hell." Austin's turn to stutter.

I'm about to confide in him but suddenly I'm scared: *what if he thinks I'm going insane!*

"Ah it's nothing!" I say in my most convincing voice. However, a slight quiver is not missed by my forever friend. I see him tense instinctively and move closer to place a protective arm on my shoulder. Never mind that this is the fifth week in a row that I've had at least a version of this dream, once per week.

This dream has somehow deviated since the first occurrence. But I'm unable to process how because Austin is speaking to me again.

"That didn't sound or look like nothing! Your face was contorting as if mirroring the images! Signaling a fear that I've never seen before!"

I vehemently insist that I'm good. He looks at me accusingly but says nothing. I chime in quickly before he is able to challenge my words.

"I am just really tired so that's why I was dreaming in colour!"

I laugh loudly at my own sad joke, which is my default reaction to any form of discomfort – laughter. Austin shakes his head as if to clear the images but seems genuinely relieved; although, he doesn't laugh along with me, not this time. Which conveys to me, his genuine concern and fear.

He says, "Are you sure you're going to be ok?"

More to appease him than anything else I suggest,

"You are welcome to sleep here, in my bed, if that makes you happy!"

He is caught off guard by this unusual request, but quickly recovers. He states:

"OK, but if you as much as breathe on me too hard, I'll skin you alive!"

We both laugh out loud this time and pretend that we're having a typical evening. I tell him to leave the light on for good measure.

A grown man, sleeping with the lights on: when did my life become so pathetic?

Chapter 2

Cyril's Secret

The next morning, I awake to the smell of bacon and burnt toast. Still that headache. I love bacon! Did I say I LOVE bacon? I take a quick shower and head downstairs to face the day, still struggling to push away the far too unsettling images of the night from hell. My head still pounding, as if all the blood in my body has been dispatched to rescue my brain from turning into mush.

Although I have been trying so very hard not to, but I have to admit this, even to myself: I have been struggling with depression over the last few months (well maybe longer). I know that Austin has sensed this and that is partly why he's here. I wonder briefly if that's the reason for the vivid dreams. I genuinely just want to feel better but I am often too exhausted to create a plan of action and execute it. I've watched my aunt deal with depression for years so at the very least I should tell someone and seek help. But every time I think about what that help would entail: doctors, hospital, drugs, it's just too massive of an undertaking for me to undertake right now. Because, in my estimation, once it is uttered; I fear it will balloon exponentially, outside of my control. And for me, a controlled existence, is the only quality of life worth having.

Plus, I hate doctors with everything that's in me. That's why I became a comedian: they prescribe drugs, that will require other drugs to repair the damage that the first drug caused; however, my drug of choice is laughter. No one has ever needed to be treated for laughter. Therefore, I go through the motions, hoping that one day I'll just snap out of this depressive state. I know this is a juvenile assumption but what else can I do?

Austin is dressed in a pair of blue jeans and a brown t-shirt: brown has always been his favourite colour. I withhold my comment as I have grown tired of discussing the lack of colour in his closet. What about red? I remember the bat and the boy in my dream so I quickly chase away the images with a question.

"What are you burning bro?"

"I'm just making sure the toast is well done!" Austin declares accompanied by his strong, manly laugh.

I laugh too but only half-heartedly. These days, everything is half-hearted which has led to my comedy being dark, but people still seem to enjoy it. My shows are always sold out. I guess I am not the only one struggling with dark thoughts these days. I don't want to think of other people's problems right now, when I don't even have the energy to process mine.

As far back as I can remember, Austin has always

made me laugh. When we played outside his house, and a bully beat me in a game or literally, he would be quick to make me laugh. Through the years we have remained close friends, strangely enough, never marrying. Who could blame us considering the families we escaped from.

Austin is an only child from a traditional nuclear family and I was raised by my aunt Felecie. His parents somehow managed to stay together until he had finished university; while, my parents died in a car crash. Well, that's not entirely accurate: my dad and step mom died in that crash, I never knew my real mom. Aunt Felecie is my only relative in Canada so she raised me and living with her was always a numbers game as there was no telling how many days I would go without being beaten. Strangely enough, I love her. She has always been my most consistent support system and everyone needs consistency in life so I came to see her abuse and sometimes neglect as a sign of love and a small price to pay for food and shelter. Let's face it, at the time I didn't see it as abuse: it was just a way of being, our way.

The other peculiarity about my aunt was that, she could go for days in a trancelike state, occasionally mumbling or shouting that *they* were coming to get us. I always wondered who *they* were until my late teen years when she was diagnosed with schizophrenia. Not just the regular, run of the mill schizophrenia, but a special type: schizoaffective disorder. This means, in addition to the typical symptoms: extreme paranoia and hallucinations – she is also chronically depressed. Hence, my apprehension in not wanting to admit that I am struggling with depression. What if I have what she has? Although I'm pretty sure that what I am experiencing is not half as bad as hers. I hope.

Growing up, I never knew what mood she would be in, on any given day neither could I predict what her actions would be from day to day. One time, it got so bad that she locked us in our apartment and made me hide under the bed for three days because she was convinced that *they* were going to get me. At that point, I really wished that *they* had come to get me. Luckily, I think the neighbours noticed that I hadn't been going to school and called the police. When they came, they removed me from under the bed and took us to the hospital to get checked. After that I stayed with Austin's mom (aunt Fiona) for a few weeks until auntie was better.

Aunt Fiona has always been there for us. Aunt Felecie was given a prescription along with a social worker; after all, she had not caused any bodily harm. At least none that was readily apparent. However, I still have a deep-seated fear of tight spaces and an inexplicable fear of everything that crawls. Because, all those days under the bed, I felt like *Gulliver in the Land of Lilliput:* I felt like little creatures, just outside my scope of vision was crawling all over me. Clearly, I am definitely no stranger to trauma so there is absolutely no way a little depression is going to deter me. Most significantly, I am male and Jamaican and Jamaicans never get depressed or at least that's what my relatives back home said when they were informed of aunt Felecie's condition. I am not entirely sure who, but I am almost sure someone had said she should just "pray more". Someone else asked, "How come she dey a foreign an depress?" Apparently, there is myth that once you land in Canada, you have access to a flowery bed of ease and contentment; as a result of, the money tree strategically grown in your back yard.

Essentially, after the childhood I've had, to keep myself from crying, I laugh. I laugh all the time, in sickness and in health. Later, when my friends asked what happened, why I had been away from school for three whole days I told them: "We went camping under my bed!"

Sure enough, someone yelled: "But you're Black! Black people never go camping!"

Someone else declared, "It's a rule!"

We all laughed and I pretended like it was all fun and games. But I knew that I had been scarred by that encounter, I could fool everyone but not myself.

Ostensibly, in any social setting, I always have the most fun of everyone. I am always the loudest. I always appear to be the happy go lucky type and I am always able to make other people laugh. Basically, laughter is a gift that I do not take lightly. Ironically, what they don't know is that I laugh to keep myself from crying because I am always more than a little fearful that I would start crying and wouldn't know how to stop. Also, growing up I was an emotional child, but I was frequently warned that a man is not supposed to cry so I swapped my sad tears, for tears of laughter. With all things considered, they are not entirely the same and the latter is inadequate to soothe me.

After high school, it came as no surprise to anyone when I chose to become a *stand-up comedian* and quite a successful one. In doing so, I seem to have mastered the fine art of ventriloquism; I am both the ventriloquist and his dummy. I've worked hard and I am at the top of game; hence, this million-dollar house which is more of a prison than a home.

Chapter 3

Austin's Assessment

Cyril says he is fine and I really want to believe him. Notwithstanding, there's something about his eyes which tells a different story. I've come to realize that the eyes never lie. I am worried that he is slipping further into depression. How can I help him if he won't let me? It's this goddamn house. He stays cooped up here all the time. His life is filled with contradictions: either he is performing at a show or he's here but in social situations he is always the life of the party. Clearly, he could easily get any girl he wants but instead he prefers to get them from the yellow pages.

This conundrum is primarily the reason I came over yesterday, an intervention of sorts. There is so much I want to say to him but despite his bravado and because of last night's episode, I am suddenly afraid to confront him. He seems like a little boy again, a little boy in a little boat, on a great big ocean; being tossed about by angry waves and howling winds. So yes, I am terribly afraid! I am terrified that one unskilfully selected word, will break my friend and brother.

My friend who has so much – but lives like he has nothing - apart from this nest he lives in. As if in some way, he thinks that he is undeserving so naturally he punishes himself as if he has taken a vow of poverty. My friend who has been through so much – who has proverbially weathered so many storms: his dad's death, his mom's abandonment, his aunt's on-going battle with mental illness and of course that other thing that we absolutely never talk about.

The problem is, although I was too young to understand this at the time, I watched my dad battle his demons and felt powerless to help. He battled them alone and was overwhelmed by them. After all, what could a kid do? Especially when you have Caribbean parents, who feel strongly that kids should be seen and not heard.

I guess to a large extent, my dad's struggle was and is different: his struggle is with the bottle. But fundamentally, he quite possibly is depressed as well which led him to the bar. I watched as alcohol ripped my family apart: he became abusive to my mom and me. I hate him! I hate to think of him as my dad and on some level, I am deathly afraid that I will become him. I will become that man who abused his wife and child. So, I vowed to remain single until I am absolutely sure that there is no trace of him in me. In my head! Because isn't that where every thing begins, in the mind. Haven't we heard from we were babies that, *what the mind can conceive can be achieved.* That's why I wear a helmet around my head, a helmet of fear to protect me from the part of me that is my dad. After all, don't we eventually become our parents?

For instance, look at Cyril, he grew up with his aunt and in some way has inherited her depression. He doesn't ever talk about it! He would never speak a negative word against the woman who raised him but the evidence is clear. No one ever talks about these things, no one warns you in Elementary school or even high school that these things could happen but take it from me, there's a growing body of evidence that points to this being true, without a shadow of a doubt. How else do we explain things, issues, situations that pass on from one generation to the next?

With all that being said, I really need to rescue Cyril but instead of fulfilling my mandate, I cook for him, well I give him burnt toast, with bacon and strawberry jam (his all-time favourite). I tell myself that I will speak to him at another time, there is always time, right? How could I have predicted what happened next?

Chapter 4

Aunt Felecie

I hear t*hem* coming! I lock all the windows; as a matter of cold fact, I strategically placed card board over the windows.

I miss my little apartment. But my nephew and son Cyril is doing great things in the world so he was able to buy this bungalow on the *other side* of town. The side of town which I have always admired: the well manicured, always green lawns, with the short apple trees and the ever-pervasive smell of lilacs. My absolutely most favourite flowers: white, violet, blue magenta. I love all the colours. I never actually thought I could or would live here but here I am. Although I do wish that Cyril would visit more. Oh well, I guess we can't have it all. No one can.

I have always derived such great pleasure in just sitting on my porch, just taking in the view of the neighbourhood, usually there's no one out and about but the scenery makes up for the absence of humans. And really a part from the people at my church, I am uncomfortable talking to anyone else. I get so anxious just thinking about talking to my neighbours. Today, I can not seem to calm myself enough to just sit outside and just look around! I have butterflies in my stomach and I can not shake the feeling that *they* are really, really, without a shadow of doubt coming to get me today. To be honest, I've always known that this day would come! I've always known that *this* day would come! I always knew that *they* would come to get me one day… my long-standing appointment with destiny. An appointment that although I did not in anyway make, I am absolutely obligated to keep.

On top of the acute anxiety (that's what my doctor calls it) I feel a great ache! An ache that I cannot describe, one that I have been feeling for a while, which has intensified. I've never really been good with words. I try to ignore the panic that creeps up on me, but sadly not today.

I've been able to trick the social worker lady, who shows up once a week, that I've been taking my meds. This is because, over the years I've been able to mimic a calm that I don't possess plus she is overworked so she is always in a hurry. I actually had a great social worker a few years ago; that time, I definitely had to take my meds but then they took her away. That was a really difficult time for me. But I survived, I always do.

My other major issue which makes me feel worse and avoid people is that I have alopecia. It is so severe that I have lost all the hair in the middle of my head, at the sides and just have fine tufts of hair, which has not grown in the last ten years. People don't actually know how important your hair is, until you don't have it anymore. Black women are always like: *I can't be bothered with my 4C hair. It's too short! It's too thick!* I would gladly accept too short or too thick, any day just so I could have a full head of hair. I don't know about anyone else but that struggle for me is as real as it gets. I was never what anyone would be quick to call a social butterfly but these days, I'm lucky if I make it to the grocery store.

When I first learned that I was losing my hair, Cyril – being the gem that he is – bought me all the expensive products, sent me to expensive specialists. Nothing helped! No one helped! No one came to save me! The story of my life! In fact, the last individual I saw was as a special favour from my family physician. I requested to be seen by a Black dermatologist because up until then, I only saw white specialists. Let's face it, what does old, white men know about Black hair? Don't get me wrong, they are always cordial, respectful and concerned but I always felt like, maybe - just maybe - they didn't have a clue what to do about my mane problem.

Needless to say, when I got the appointment (quite expeditiously) to see a Black specialist: I was overjoyed! On the appointed day, I woke up early, washed the little hair I had left and put products on my scalp – not too much – for fear that he might not approve. After all, no matter the circumstances, a lady must always look her best.

I walked in, saw the degrees on his wall (this guy even

had awards) needless to say; I felt like I was finally in the right place, at the right time and seeing the right person. I came to see this as my *Cornelius meeting* because I already had imagined that by the end of the day, I would have been using the right products or doing the right procedure. I felt for sure that my prayers were finally being answered and that God was finally working in my favour! Because I had been in enough *"name it and claim it services"*, enough *lines of prophecy, touched and agreed with all my neighbours, done told my neighbours that it was finish,* been covered in enough olive oil *to* not know that it was my time for a miracle, for a breakthrough. Yes, I felt like there was a *miracle in the room, with my name on it.*

Therefore, when Mr. Expert said, "Let me see your hair!"

Because of course I wore my most fancy wig. I never left my house without my wig. So much so, that I live in mortal fear of dying, not because I'm afraid of going to the darkest hell, but because of the fear that my wig will fall off. I am crippled by the fear of losing my wig in public even at church. In all those many and various lines, I'd be first in line, holding on to my wig for dear life. Most people at my church don't even know that I wear wigs; despite, the fact that I've fellowshipped with them for years. Somethings, you just don't discuss. It will be to your shame for lacking faith.

Can you imagine my surprise when Mr. Professional said, "Don't even sit down! Because there is nothing I can do for you. Your hair loss is too far gone. There's nothing I can do for you except point you in the direction of a very good wig specialist". I was beyond speechless.

He said it just like that, no malice, no malevolence, just like that. Can you imagine my disappointment? I was crushed! I was angry! I was beyond disappointed! I was disillusioned! What exactly do you do when the people who are supposed to help you, the specialists, are out of options? What do you do when you don't know what to do? How can you know if no one explains it to you?

I was so depressed, even more than before. You know that advertisement about a medication for depression, where the little guy is walking under a dark cloud; that was me and I was him! That became my life, all day, everyday. Slowly, days turned into weeks, and weeks turned into months and months turned to years and just like that: acceptance. Clearly, somehow, and for some strange reason, the God who makes hair everyday, had decided that I was to go around, buried and lost in a sea of hair: without hair. And that's how it felt everyday that I was drowning in a sea of hair. Everyone around me has beautiful hair: black girls, white girls, Indian girls, even Chinese girls who can't seem to do much with their hair. Of course, I did what all zealots do, I beseeched God and when that failed, I bargained with Him; when that too failed, I boycotted His services. However, I soon discovered that I greatly missed the human interaction so I went back to church. No new growth for me, no big chop experience either. But there's an inexplicable beauty in acceptance, there's a lightening of the load, a deep and settled peace.

Naturally, being the rational person, I am, I endeavoured to ascertain the unique lesson in my predicament. Because isn't it true that when we go through an experience it becomes personal; we become one with the experience and we feel that we are the only ones called to carry this load? Sometimes we even feel like we are the experience. Also, I believe in that sense of community where each one teaches one. I also figured that I had lost so many things that I loved, so many people as well, so why would a great God take my hair. Obviously, there is a lesson in this.

Intermittently, lessons started to emerge because if you look long and hard enough you will make discoveries; real or imagined, even if it's from your own fabrication. I documented each lesson for posterity.

Lessons in Hair
1. I was placed in this process/situation to learn a few things that I might not have learned otherwise.
2. One can neither rush nor circumvent the process.
3. There are no short cuts through/around or in the process. It doesn't matter how much you fast, pray, speak in tongues, fall out in the spirit: there's no alternate route.
4. You learn about your self in the process: strengths, weaknesses and your uniqueness.
5. You discern who your true friends are in the process; also, you learn that some friends are just acquaintances and that some people are frenemies.
6. The Word of God is fulfilled in your life through this process because you see life lessons clearly in the scriptures and through other people's lived experiences.
7. Always be grateful for all you have, as that could be

taken at anytime; remember Job, remember Lot's wife. An attitude of gratitude is paramount.
Examples:
- ❖ The woman with the issue of blood (Lk. 8. 43-58. KJV). A state of continuous uncleanness leading to social isolation. She therefore learns that her money was inadequate. That sometimes you need things that money cannot buy.
- ❖ The man at pool who had no one to assist him in getting in the pool for healing to happen (St. In. 5. 1-9, KJV). No friends, no family, again faced with social isolation.
- ❖ Paul's thorn in his flesh (2nd Cor. 12. 7-10). Verse ten is rich in paradox: weakness and strength juxtaposed, able vs. disabled transposed. Paul learns to identify his strengths and weaknesses as well.

8. The process is an occasion to count and accumulate blessings.

Based on my discovery, I feel like I'm in good company, amongst the elite of scripture; therefore, I have learned to accept the things that I am powerless to change. However, today I feel a change coming: I am more anxious than I've ever been. I even feel the urge to take my pills.

Chapter 5
A Time to Die

I take a few of my pills, you know, to make up for the days when I didn't feel like taking any. After a few hours, I feel super chill, you know like relaxed. I thought, why not take a few more, for good measure. By then I am floating. Before long, I have taken close to half of the amount in my bottle. I start to feel not so chill. All the voices are quiet, they've just vanished, the first time in how many years. Why have I not been taking my pills before now? The problem is though, when the voices stop, then I am alone.

Prior to today, I was never alone. I had those voices to speak to me, some in different accents, sometimes they spoke horrifying things; things that left me quivering and whimpering in a corner. Doctrines that should never be uttered. This is the fundamental reason I stopped taking my pills. It is neither the numbness, nor the oblivion that I despise; it is the silence. I am always able to live alone in sickness and in health because I always had the company of those voices. But they are quiet today, exceptionally quiet, so quiet that I think my world has ended.

Pretty soon, I am overshadowed by languor, not the exhausted type but the slow type that sneaks up on you and brings with it that sweet sense of being tranquil, which washes over you and immediately take you straight to REM sleep. Sleep's quiet presence sits in the room, is gently wrapped around my legs, then without much fanfare, crawls through my body, crippling me. Surprisingly, for the first time ever, I am able to literally see myself. It is as if I were seeing myself for the very first time, like really see myself. It is funny that after all these years of living in this body, I still don't know myself. Fundamentally, while growing up, they instruct you to love everyone, forgive all perceived wrongs but they never tell you to love and forgive yourself. No, they never show you how worthy you are of love and forgiveness. They never tell you that despite your imperfections that you are enough. They leave you to figure it out on your own and by then, you are way past your prime. Hence, some of us never discover our true self, our full potential. It's like the song says, *"I've been to paradise but I've never been to me!"*

I hear a sound and I look towards it and it's my dear, dear friend Zimera. She looks at me knowingly. I say, "Hi dear" but not with my voice. She hears me though, she always hears me. She says, "How are you feeling today?" Again, I respond in my mind, "Oh, I've had better days".

"You just rest now Felecie. Everything is going to be fine!"

This time when I speak, I find my voice, "Please take care of Cyril because he's all I have in this world!"

She quietly says, "You know I will".

Zimera's presence has always been so soothing.

I remember vividly the first time she came. I was in a really bad way. I had just moved into this house, to this neighbourhood and I was feeling so overwhelmed, out of my depths. I thought I was going to die. As usual, the panic attack showed itself. It always shows up when I am alone and scared. Slowly, Zimera stepped into my room. I should have been more afraid of a strange woman in my house, but I wasn't. Even then, I knew she was my answered prayer. From that time, we've been friends. To be honest, sometimes, I am not sure if she is real or imagined. I don't trouble myself about those things anymore. Why? When realities are amplified based on your level of consciousness. All I know is, I need her and she shows up. Isn't that the very definition of friendship?

I allow the darkness to overwhelm me. How could I fight against this resounding sense of peace and tranquility that I've never known before? For the first time ever, I am not afraid, I have a complete sense of who I am and I am simultaneously unafraid and unashamed. I do what comes naturally, I close tired eyes, and give way to the darkness and the calmness of the moment.

I hope Cyril will forgive me for leaving him behind. I hope he knows how much I have always and will always love him.

All the while listening to the birds chirping in the distance.

Chapter 6

The Fallout

I notice a few missed calls from an unfamiliar number so after the fifth time, I answer it. The voice, a woman's voice says,

"Hi my name is Maxine Perth and I'm calling from the hospital." I instantly perk up, "Yes".

I didn't get to ask which one.

"Are you Austin Blane?"

"Yes".

I go through the motions of confirming my identity, stating my full name, date of birth, full address and my mom's name. I anxiously await an explanation for all this. I want to hear yet I don't want to hear. It's going to be bad. I can already tell. My palms are sweating and my mouth is dry.

Maxine continues, "We have you listed here as an emergency contact for Felecie Parks. Her primary contact, Cyril Parks is not answering".

I said, "Yes, she's a close family friend. Is she ok? Cyril, her son, is on business out of town for the day".

Then in a very calm, matter of fact tone, she says something that changes our worldview forever.

"Usually, we don't do this kind of thing over the phone, but there.... there are mitigating circumstances. I'm afraid that I have to inform you that Ms. Parks has died of a suspected overdose. We need someone to ID the body so we can get her on the list to do an emergency autopsy because she was under a doctor's care. Apparently, the last time she saw him (I can tell that she is checking her notes) was last week Tuesday, the 7th. She was fine at the time so we have to rule out medical issues".

While she speaks of what can only be described as a misunderstanding, a complete and utter misdiagnosis. Surely, they are talking about someone else. She has just described to me another family's agony.

To connect with something real and ordinary, to get my bearings back, I look through my office window, as I've done a thousand times before. It is such a calm, beautiful spring day here in Toronto. The sun is out in all her glory, not a single cloud in the sky. In everyway that counts, a beautiful day. There is no indication, nothing prophesying of the deluge that is about to overwhelm us. I see a bird's nest across the way. I have been watching it for a while now, from construction started. It houses a bird family; apparently today is fledgling day as the mother bird, pushes her baby bird out the nest. She watches calmly as he tries to fly and swoops down to break his fall – I can't see the ground – but I assume, she catches him before he falls. I can't help but wonder, who is going to catch Cyril now before he falls? Who is going to be his mama bird?

A thousand questions flood my mind but unyieldingly my mouth doesn't work. Why won't my lips move? Eventually, I extricate my voice and ask when and where this madness happened. Because that's exactly what this is: complete and utter insanity. How could sweet aunt Felecie be dead? How could Bible touting, fire and brimstone shouting aunt Felecie do this horrible thing to herself – to us! How could she of all persons kill herself? Sometimes, this world just does not make any good sense!

Maxine pauses for a few minutes, then wishes me a great day and declares how sorry she is, sorry for our loss. Cyril's loss! She hangs up! My head is spinning. What's going to happen to Cyril now? Absolutely no good can come in the wake of this, it will only serve to push him over the edge. I feel awful for my friend; however, this is a loss for me as well. I have always loved aunt Felecie. She is eccentric in many ways but she is always kind. I'm quick to correct myself: I mean was. She always embodied a childlike innocence while being fiercely intelligent. An intelligence that sometimes glowed in her eyes despite or maybe in spite of her long battle with mental illness.

I brush away a rash tear from my left eye as I decide on a course of action. Cyril is going to need my support now more than ever. My paramount objective is to let him know what has happened, that his sole custodian for so many years has transitioned. This is not going to be easy but, I take solace in the fact that he will hear this from me and not a stranger.

I quietly pray that my tongue does not lose its shrewdness.

Cyril

It's still early June and usually Syracuse, New York is beautiful this time of year, beaming with bright sunshine. I love driving here as the green, dense trees, rolling hills and streams remind me of my first home, Gayle, St. Mary, Jamaica. It's funny how the mind works, because while I don't have a clear memory of my grand parents, their house, etc. I have a very vivid memory of their surroundings. These surroundings which have left an indelible mark in my mind; so much so, that my house is nestled among trees and sits on land that mirrors this part of my memory. I guess that's why I love trees. They are always comforting regardless of what is going on in my world. It's a good thing that memories don't leave us like people do.

There are various types of trees in Syracuse (I Googled it) they vary in colour, shape and sizes. The colourful and short Amur Maple, the Sugar Maple and the Red Oak which actually blossoms; from a pale shade of pink into a bright red. That being said, Syracuse is also known for having a lot of snow in the winter. They can get up to 124 inches of snowfall on average. It's spring here now though, not quite summer yet so I am happy to get this gig at the Landmark Theatre. A beautiful historic building with beautiful murals, which are reminiscent of 18th century architecture.

Today, it is not as beautiful as I had wished. It is raining all kinds of wild animals, lightning and thunder. I feel miserable. Despite being from the Caribbean where there is frequent rainfall in the hurricane season, I hate the rain. It reminds me of tears and in my life, I have been acquainted with enough; therefore, I don't need any reminders. In my line of work, there is no room for tears except those brought on by immeasurable and sustained laughter.

So here I am, driving in the rain, hating to put on the heat but I have to because it's cold rain. I try to banish the misery which threatens to overwhelm me. I turn on the radio to brighten my mood, and I sigh because as fate would have it, one of those really sad 70s or 80s songs is playing which use to be one of aunt Felecie's favourite (before she found Jesus, hymns and the Psalmist) "... *but I wish someone had talked to me like I want to talk to you…..I've been to paradise but I've never been to me*". This seems to have been the soundtrack to her life. A song about the loss of self and purpose and an innate desire to be someone else.

Thankfully, my phone rings and it's Austin. I don't generally take calls while I'm driving especially since this is a rental and it's not in sync with my phone. I answer, just to hear a friendly voice in the gloom. But I should have just listened to the song because that's a type of manufactured grief that I can tolerate. Nothing could have prepared me for Austin's news.

Aunt Felecie is dead! My aunt Felecie! This is insane! There must be some mistake here. I reason that it is one of two things: Austin did not hear correctly; hence, I have not heard accurately. By the time I get back to the T-dot, this mess would have been sorted out.

After Austin hangs up, at first, I laugh and tell myself that it's a prank. But I've never known Austin to lie about anything this serious or even sound this down in the dumps. I do what I often do when the harsh realities of life overwhelm me – I escape into my fantasy realm - where I am the hero and my word is law. Immediately, I'm there where my mom is loving and attentive and my dad, brave and dependable. He slays dragons and calms the angry seas. My siblings are loyal and selfless and they travel to far away kingdoms to bring me my bride. Today, I struggle to hold on to these images. I can't keep a grip on my escapist vision. My reality is too harsh and all consuming. I can not disassociate from the moment, nothing can or will comfort me. Nothing will ever be the same again. Just like the pouring rain, prickly tears threaten to overpower and devastate me. I refuse to give in; after all, a grown man is not supposed to cry.

Plus, everyone knows that the show must go on. It's a huge struggle and a battle rages within me all through the show. I tell them the story of the Jamaican man who discovers that all his six children were fathered by another man and he sits in the bar crying and the waiter asks, "What happen to you boss?" He tells the waiter his plight and the waiter who is truly Jamaican declares, *"A six jacket you one affi wear, bredda a how you so careliss. That couldn't happen to me! Me ongly have two"*. In Jamaica, a child who has been given to the wrong father is called *a jacket*. Everyone laughs in all the right places. I even pause to have a good laugh myself. Soon after meeting and greeting my fans, taking too many selfies and signing t-shirts and any available surface, it's time to catch the late flight back to Canada. To face my nightmare.

When we just moved to Canada, we lived in Whitby, on Tallships, next to the infamous mental hospital. I'm not even sure if it's still there, it's been a while since we left. Aunt Felecie always enjoyed being out in the boonies, we both did. That reminds me of the unpleasantness that lies ahead. Oh, how am I ever going to get through this? How am I ever going to be whole again, when I wasn't even whole to begin with? My aunt taught me many valuable lessons, like how to be a man, how to be honest and true, how to look out for myself because no one else will; however, she never taught me how to live without her near. Guess, I am going to have to learn and quickly too. Because now I am going to be less whole, like a quarter of a half. I wonder how much wholeness that equates to. Math was never my strong suit.

I feel that stupid headache threatening.

It's funny how the mind works. Essentially, things that you think you might have forgotten or deemed unremarkable, garner strength, amass reverence when significant others have been extricated from our lives, without warning or build up. On the flight back home, I remember the very last conversation I had with my aunt. It was her birthday and I went to see her. I don't always get a chance to but I do try to see her on her birthday; at any rate, I did. I remember sitting in her neat, tastefully decorated living room, with the smell of lilacs wafting in the air. After the obligatory candle deflaming (if there is such a term) moment, aunt Felecie did something that she doesn't usually do. She asked me about my life. We normally like to keep it light when I visit but, on that occasion, she was very specific about wanting to, no needing to know how my life was going. It was a simple question yet the weight of it, is now magnified.

She said, "How are things *wid* (with) you baby?

I responded like I always do. "I am great auntie! Things are going really well".

To be clear, in this family, we hardly talk about feelings and emotions neither is there any prying. Also, there is little room for small talk and things like that.

She went on to declare:

"I hope you are happy baby. That is all I have ever wanted for you! Because having a lot of money or friends, does not bring contentment. You can have all the trimmings that the world can afford but what's the point if your soul is maxed out!"

In retrospect, there were so many nuggets that she was offering me, so many signals, a point of entry to initiate a discussion and I missed them all. Was my aunt telling me goodbye? Was she telling me that her soul was maxed out? Foolishly, I saw it as one of her hyper-religious pronouncements. I should have paid more attention to her comment, to her, but sadly its too late now.

The magnitude of that moment and the current is just too much. Yet, as always, through force of habit, sheer will power, being among so many strangers, I don't know exactly what it is but I reigned in my emotions and willed away the tears that were a threat to my well-being. Ever since I was a kid, I could always identify the exact moments when the cloud of my emotions was about to explode and strong arm them into fleeing.

I refuse to fold though! I have to be strong or even pretend to be strong for aunt Felecie, I am not going to lie, it's not going to be easy especially because the details surrounding her death is cloudy at best. Maybe, there's been a mistake. Just maybe it's someone else's auntie and not mine. After all mistakes like these happen all the time. Don't they?

I say a silent prayer into the dark night. Nothing will ever be the same again.

Chapter 7

The Funeral

Sometimes, in your life everything is just normal and you are sick of the same ole, same ole. But during times of hardships, all you want is the normal, the routine, the boring, the same ole same ole. Sameness is a very underrated luxury.

Somehow, the preparations for the funeral are made. The days before go by in a haze. I am both dazed and confused, like I've been hit in the head and kicked in the stomach. I am eternally grateful to Austin and auntie Fiona.

On the day of the funeral it rains all day; not a down pour of such, but a very cold and steady rain. My mind keeps doing all these crazy flips, alternating from the past to the present. A past that I have simultaneously tried to escape yet feel a compulsion to visit time after time.

I remember one of my aunt's favourite sayings, she always said *if it rains on the day of a funeral, the dearly departed was not ready to leave.* I guess she was not ready to die. I'm not ready to say goodbye either – so many things left unsaid – so many things implied but never specifically stated. I feel so much guilt for not spending more time with the most constant human in my life. One more thing to add to my list of guilt. But by the same token, I'm angry. How could she leave me, just when I need her the most! Just like all the other adults in my life have done, abandon me!

The rituals of the service go by in a blur. I am still dazed and confused. How do I make sense of all this? How does anyone make sense of death? Today a loved one is here, you can call them, hear them breathing on the other end of the line, imagine a smile at your greeting and a laugh at your comments; but tomorrow they could be in a box at the front of a church: not breathing, not smiling, no sound of laughter and not able to smell their favourite flowers. There are so many moving parts to this narrative that doesn't make any sense. Aunt Felecie *should* be at church (she loves church…loved church) not me. I have not been to church in years, yet here we all are. Not that I don't believe in God or accept the teachings of the Church but for too long there have been too many disparities: where many so-called Ministers of the Gospel, preach like Paul but are as bitter as Saul.

Before long, after the singing of hymns and the reading of auntie's favourite scripture, Romans 8: 18-28

[18] *I consider that our present sufferings are not worth comparing with the glory that will be revealed in us.* [19] *For the creation waits in eager expectation for the chil-*

dren of God to be revealed. [20] *For the creation was subjected to frustration, not by its own choice, but by the will of the one who subjected it, in hope* [21] *that the creation itself will be liberated from its bondage to decay and brought into the freedom and glory of the children of God.*

[22] *We know that the whole creation has been groaning as in the pains of childbirth right up to the present time.* [23] *Not only so, but we ourselves, who have the first fruits of the Spirit, groan inwardly as we wait eagerly for our adoption to sonship, the redemption of our bodies.* [24] *For in this hope we were saved. But hope that is seen is no hope at all. Who hopes for what they already have?* [25] *But if we hope for what we do not yet have, we wait for it patiently.*

[26] *In the same way, the Spirit helps us in our weakness. We do not know what we ought to pray for, but the Spirit himself intercedes for us through wordless groans.* [27] *And he who searches our hearts knows the mind of the Spirit, because the Spirit intercedes for God's people in accordance with the will of God.*

[28] *And we know that in all things God works for the good of those who love him, who have been called according to his purpose.*

She was an eternal optimist. Austin nudges me. It is my turn – my turn to deliver a final tribute to my beloved aunt. This is really going to be hard.

I share the usual with the congregants; mostly her church folks and aunt Fiona's friends: aunt Felecie's full name, date of birth, schools attended, career, favourite songs, some of her struggles; raising me like her own. By struggles I mean, immigrant struggles, nothing that would defame her. I make them laugh as well since that is what I do; by telling them about my escapades while growing up and my auntie's often hilarious response. In my mind, I decide that she will have two services: this public event and the one in my heart.

The hard part is the burial – the finality of the custom

breaks my heart – this is really the end. They throw dirt on her box, but not me, I give her, her favourite flowers for the last time – lilacs. The reverend declares, *"dust to dust, ashes to ashes"*. It is over! My aunt is gone forever.

Everything happens in slow motion but at the same time goes by really quickly.

At the end, Austin hugs me and say, "You did well! Auntie would be proud".

It is really weird how Austin is always aware of what I need; exactly, when I need it.

Chapter 8

Unstated Truths

Felecie Parks was born second of two children, her brother Vince being the older. All her life she had been second to Vince, the invincible. He had been a rambunctious child who feared no one and grew up to be an impetuous man without a social conscience. His good looks and natural athleticism made him quite popular with the ladies and he seemingly could do no wrong for his parents.

Indeed, he was the golden child who was quite privileged in a number of ways: first, he was male and second, he had the right complexion (light brown) in post colonial Jamaica. Vince was quite skilled at handling a football which soon earned him a place among Jamaica's elite *Reggae Boys* and he was poised for greatness. However, true to his nature, his lack of discipline manifested itself as he soon grew bored and decided that he wanted to go abroad. Sometimes, Felecie believed that whatever Vince wanted, he just had to voice it and then the universe would deliver on a platter. But, not her – definitely not her. She had to work hard to prove herself – always had to prove that she was worthy – and even after proving herself, the struggle was still real.

Vince had been involved in a number of failed relationships and was now panicking because he had started to feel old and unaccomplished. Not withstanding, he left his girlfriend with a baby. Vince Parks migrated to Canada to ostensibly attend university but soon discovered that his life was not as grand as he wanted it to be. Therefore, not wanting to return to Jamaica empty handed, he decided to fine a nice girl to settle down with and make babies as well. By nice he meant a fan who was fanatical about him and meeting his needs; as usual, the universe delivered. After all, the way he saw it, if you are a proper man, you have to have children.

He met and fell in love with Tanya Jenkins, the first of three children and the only girl. This made her the perfect candidate; as a result of, her natural ability to take charge of a situation. This tendency suited Vince just fine, after all he was still a child - a man child. Also, she was a very successful financial advisor so Vince was in heaven.

As fate would have it, after the marriage he discovered that the love of his life could not conceive. Tanya was devastated and wept for months. But being the fighter that she had always been, she soon bounced back from her disappointment. She always knew that she would carry this sadness, this unfairness; the knowledge that her womb had failed her. Her own body had betrayed her. They hastily put in the paperwork for Cyril to relocate to Canada. By then, Cyril was living with aunt Felecie because his mom had dropped him off when he was two months old and hadn't been heard from since. Felecie didn't mind much because she had, had no prospects of marriage and she was already taking care of her aging parents.

Shortly, after submitting the paperwork, young Cyril came to Canada at the age of three, March 24, 1992 with his aunt Felecie, his primary caregiver, as both his dad and stepmom had to work. After all, this is Canada everyone has to work. He spent all his formative years with his aunt and grew to understand her idiosyncrasies and loved her regardless. Obviously, this is not to say that Tanya didn't love him but he was a tangible reminder of her inadequacy so gradually she spent less and less time with him. Plus, Cyril looks so much like his dad – the man she loved and wanted so desperately to please – that sometimes it hurt to look at him. Despite her own sadness, she always ensured that all Cyril's needs were met. Also, she was scared to death of being rejected by him so she mostly lived on the periphery of his life, trying not to hover.

Tanya was always happy that she had sent for Felecie as well – calm, well possessed Felecie, who was always happy to help. Many wintry evenings she would come home to find them huddled together in front of the stone fireplace. Not withstanding, on December 24th a year after Cyril had been in Canada, when they were invited to a Christmas eve party Tanya thought they were lucky to have Felecie to take care of their child; because everyone knows that child care is expensive. Never mind that no one even thought to invite Felecie to the party. Plus, little Cyril didn't seem to mind; not at all, as he had grown accustomed to spending all his time with his aunt.

When the call came at 1a.m. that Vince and his wife Tanya had been killed by a drunk driver, Felecie was devastated, as they were her sponsors; however, Cyril was oblivious to this life changing event. Shortly, after this news, Felecie discovered that Vince and his flashy wife had been living a lie. They were drowning in debt and even before the funeral, Felecie and Cyril had to leave their home, with the beautiful stone fireplace. Of course, there was no insurance because why would Vince think of doing something so selfless. Plus, a lot of Jamaicans are quite suspicious of insurance policies and everything that they entail. To her credit, Tanya did try to persuade Vince, but he convinced her that everything would be fine, "nuh worry yuself man, yu worry to much". Those were his exact words to her, to not worry.

Those were difficult times for Felecie Parks as she had to navigate a whole new world. Finding a place for them seemed difficult at first but then why would it be easy, her life had never been easy. Why would it start now? Soon she was made aware of social assistance and was able to procure a place for her and her ward and also attend college. This was indeed a huge change for her, being in a strange land, with strange customs and people who were very strange in their worldview. In her little community of Gayle, St. Mary everyone and everything was familiar to her. For starters, everyone knows everyone by name (in most instances by an alias or a Pet name). Almost everyone in the community of Gayle is an aunt or an uncle, or a cousin; despite, not being related by blood. Suddenly, she had to get use to people who neither looked like her nor did they speak her language.

Aunt Felecie being inherently resilient eventually found a part time job (she was able to take Cyril with her) and an apartment with help from the Government of Canada. The apartment was extremely small, a far cry from the lavish home that they had lost, but it was comfortable. It was their new home and it was warm in the winter, cool in the summer and always well lit. Felecie had to get use to this new country on the double, as she could not return to St. Mary empty handed. She would be the *talk* of her small community, nope the shame would have been too great. Felecie persevered and obtained a diploma in Social Work and eventually a Bachelor's degree, all while caring for Cyril.

It therefore came as no surprise to anyone when she started acting strangely. She had been placed in a position where she had to do so much, she had very little time for self care. After all, she had been programmed to take care of everyone but not herself. She complained to her friend Fiona about all the people who were stalking her, spies working for the Jamaican government who wanted to kidnap and take her back to Jamaica. Over the years, she had developed an irrational fear of being deported to Jamaica despite being able to put down roots, build a life and make a few friends. She had worked hard and had overcome seemingly insurmountable odds and was finally doing well. But isn't this the great irony of life? People work extremely hard to make a living but sometimes they are unable to enjoy their labour due to unforeseen circumstances.

Clearly, there was no way Felecie could have gone through all she did and come out unscathed. That is not how life usually works, that is not the way of the human experience. That is just not how the world is situated. Quite frankly, she had given up her dream of being a nurse to raise Cyril. This she didn't mind as much as she thought she would. However, she couldn't help but feel the way she did as a child, when Vince was fed first while she was fed the crumbs. Vince was always the super star for her parents. They often beat her for the slightest offence while Vince was never punished but allowed to be wild and free. Later, when she asked her mother why, her mom claimed, it was for her own protection but clearly Felecie had needed protection from her own parent. Her mom also asserted, "girls could get into trouble yu know" by this she meant get pregnant. Felecie wondered about the boys who could get girls pregnant, shouldn't something be done about them as well?

As a consequence, Felecie's accomplishments seemed more the consolation prize as this was never the life she dreamed of, neither the way her story was supposed to unfold. Sometimes, Felecie felt like her mother's prophecy had come to pass as she was frequently warned in childhood that she would never *"come to anything "*. Therefore, despite that or because of that, she had always pushed herself pass the limits of human endurance to make something of herself.

Ironically, on top of everything she had going on, she also had to take care of her ailing parents (financially). Parents who were never content with anything she did, nothing was enough. She wasn't enough. Naturally, she spent her whole life seeking to be validated by those around her. Invariably, with all the pressure thrusted on her: social, emotional and financial; strong, reliable Felecie started to lose her grip on reality – little by little, one day at a time.

Another huge unfulfilled dream, was to get married and have a family of her own. Sure, there were a few viable candidates here and there but nothing lasting. Felecie being a hopeless romantic kept waiting for her prince to come and rescue her from a world that was sometimes too harsh, too cold. Eventually, she had to accept that not all movies have a fairy-tale ending so she accepted that no one was coming to save her. Just like how no one saved her from her teachers' destructive tongue, her mother's wrath and the sense of abandonment she felt after Vince died: no one was ever going to save her, not now, not ever. She had to save herself, she had to choose to do this each and everyday so that like muscle memory she started to choose *her* everyday. This was an extremely painful epiphany and just as long as it took her to create this fantasy of demons, dragons and princely rescues, it took her just as long to mourn her fairy-tale world, vanishing, just drifting away.

That's when she discovered Jesus. He resonated with her rescue fantasies. She frequently declared, "Jesus found her right on time and snatched her just like a branch from the burning". Cyril never quite understood any of that and did not ask in fear of being met with an even more ambiguous retort. Cyril saw that Jesus made her happy so he was ok with Him. Little by little, Cyril saw that his aunt was drifting further and further away from him and he soon realized that some things were bigger than him so there was nothing he could do but wait and watch for the proverbial shoe to drop.

Gradually, she adopted to her new life and lived by herself for years in a new home that Cyril had bought her. Up until her death she had attended church meetings and was apart of her local assembly's choir ministry where she made a few friends. Her dream of seeing Cyril mature and excel in life was accomplished so she died happy and somewhat fulfilled as he was her number one project.

Chapter 9

Cyril's Burden

Cyril does not remember much of his parents; however, he soon came to realize what their absence meant; moving and less food – greater instability in every way. Greater instability, until auntie had found a little apartment in Brampton. Looking back, Cyril started to realize that the signs of his aunt's precariousness had been present from very early. For instance, he vividly remembers at least one time when he was five or maybe six, when she got him ready for school then promptly left. She left him in the apartment all day and didn't remember him until she came home from work. That time, she wept like a child and promised to never allow that to happen again. However, it happened a few more times and then she would become angry and punish him for her absent mindedness. It's funny how people hurt the ones they love the most and sometimes punish their loved ones for *their* own mistakes. As a matter of fact, it was during one of her moments of being distracted that Cyril met Austin and his mom when he was in grade two. Once again, Felecie had forgotten to pick him up on time and Austin's mom, who worked as a secretary at their school, understanding the situation, took him home; rather than, calling the police. She didn't like to call the police in these situations because she felt that the police would not understand the plight of a fellow Black mom, doing the best she could, in far less than ideal circumstances.

Fiona brought Cyril home and he officially met Austin whom he had seen in school but never spoke with since Austin is obviously his junior. Pretty soon, it became a routine for auntie Fiona to take home both boys when Felecie was running late. Cyril really enjoyed going home with aunt Fiona, to her comfortable town house, which was annex to a park and there was also a small garden that she tended in the spring and summer months. Cyril became a fixture at their house as he spent most evenings there and holidays as well.

On evenings, while waiting for aunt Felecie to pick him up, both boys spent the time playing games of one kind or another. Austin did not have a video game console as his mom felt that a video game would rob him of his creative. She would then go on to tell him stories of her childhood, of how she played a number of outdoor games and she didn't die. Austin realized that it was useless to press the point because her mind was already made up. Also, it was even more pointless to ask his dad because he always said no. Austin had to learn to be creative from he was really young and often played alone and grew to enjoy his time alone but having Cyril there was a bonus because two heads are definitely better than one. They played all kinds of games: card games, hide and seek, a special one they made up - *Find the Word* – where one player would stand in place and could not move until he had spelt all the words on a list that they had made together. The words would be randomly selected.

Little Austin stopped playing that game all together as he came to realize that Cyril was an excellent player because of his impeccable memory and huge vocabulary from all the time he had spent alone and had; therefore, learnt how to entertain himself by reading everything he could lay his hands on.

With everything going on at home, Cyril couldn't wait to graduate high school to move out and leave his aunt's cramped apartment. Certainly, he loved her, always would but he didn't quite understand her, not at all; plus, he was also anxious to start his own life. So far, so much of his life had been spent just living his aunt's life. He felt that it was his moment, his time to leave his mark on the world so the first chance he got, he ran. He ran and never looked back. Clearly, university was completely out of the question; despite, the fact that he would have wanted to go but aunt Felecie did not have the funds to send him as they had lived such a hand to mouth existence, occasionally robbing Peter to pay Paul. Sure, he could have applied for OSAP (Ontario Student Assistance Program) but that would simply mean a lifetime of debt. Cyril sometimes felt guilty for leaving his aunt, knowing that she wasn't always lucid but the way he had rationalized it, is that he had to leave to make a way for both of them. Aunt Felecie had lost her job some time ago because of her mental health issues.

After high school, he had looked into many options and tried many jobs, from being a valet at an upscale Toronto hotel, to driving Uber, working in restaurants and factories. Sometimes he had two and three jobs. Once he worked at a private club where they had nightly performances and among the entertainers were Stand Up Comedians. He really enjoyed their quick wit, social commentary and their ability to engage with an audience. After his first encounter with this art form, he spent a few years honing his talent and pretty soon he was in demand all across the GTA. He has always been great with words, very skilled at spinning tales; along with, the facial expression and the antics to make people laugh. In the early stages of being a comedian, he discovered that it was easy to convince club owners to allow him to perform as long he performed for free. He quickly built a fan base in the Toronto area. Life was good and he was enjoying himself.

Cyril made good money in Toronto but sometimes it was a dangerous way to live. Sometimes there would be a shooting or a stabbing and the police would shutdown the club for days at a time. Also, sometimes he would attend Raves in the basement of a building and there would be some type of altercation among party goers. At one point, he heard through the grapevine from other comedians that it was easier to make a living in the

U.S.

There was just one problem – Cyril now had a girlfriend. A girl of Middle Eastern ancestry whom he had met at one of the clubs, he was performing in. Her name was Manpreet but she preferred Preet. Unfortunately, they had to keep their relationship a secret because her parents would never approve of her dating a Black boy. There was no malice in it, just a matter of preference and a cultural expectation that at some point she would be betrothed to someone of their choosing. It's just a way of being that is culturally understood. As a matter of cold fact, she should not have been dating anyone as she had been engaged to a boy "back home" since they were fifteen years old. She had never met him but her parents had made all the arrangements so it was a done deal. Moreover, since her parents were paying for her university education, she couldn't very well not comply with them; especially, since *Nang and Namoos (honour/pride)* was at stake. Also, she would never openly disregard with her *Baba Jan* (term of endearment for her dad).

Preet figured that she would bide her time until she graduated, then get a job and disappear, go somewhere, maybe out West or to the States with Cyril. However, there is a Yiddish proverb which says: *"If you want to make God laugh, just tell Him your plan"*. Also, being a Psychology major, she knew it was a pipe dream but a girl could dream, couldn't she!

Meanwhile, Cyril was working hard so that they could build a future together. Some weeks they barely got to see each other because she had school and he had work; plus, he had his aunt to check up on ever so often. Some days she missed him so badly that it hurt to breathe but she comforted herself with the knowledge that eventually they would be together forever. She convinced herself that they would get married regardless of what her parents desired. The way she calculated it, eventually they would have a family, two kids: a son who she would call Cecil – because why not – and a daughter she would call Sybil. She had recently read a novel and the main character, Sybil was brave, confident, strong and defiant. All the things Preet decided that she wasn't. She would ensure that her only daughter had all these qualities.

One night after they had been dating for a few years, it was one of those times when they hadn't seen each other for a while. They had a reckless moment. They had been cautious for so long, hiding their relationship, monitoring how far they could go and being extremely careful; so much so, that they threw all caution to the wind. Which is quite easy to do when you spend a life time being cautious: Cyril around aunt Felecie and Preet around her family. She even had to be cautious around some of her friends as not everyone could be trusted with a secret as dangerous as hers. Indeed, she was in way too deep and was living dangerously.

In the end, none of them had expected things to unfold the way they did because after all there is a certain amount of immortality afforded to the young. Of such, life was meant to be lived salaciously and ecstatically while you're still young. They could not have imagined the chain wreck of events that later ensued. At first, Preet being young and active felt like she was just *late*, nothing to worry about. Then later, she really started to worry but it was too late as she was almost three months pregnant. She had gotten away with it for so long because she was very petite. In due time; however, she had to admit it to herself and tell Cyril. That was a really difficult conversation. She said, "I don't know how else to say this".

He said, "Babe, you're frightening me, just say it!" "Are you breaking up with me?"

She took a deep breath, swallowed hard and said, "Baby, I'm pregnant!"

He was flabbergasted, Cyril with his huge vocabulary (Mr. I know words) was beyond speechless. How could this have happened? How could she be pregnant? How could they be parents? Cyril felt like he needed to be fathered himself. They went back and forth for a few more weeks and before they knew it, her once trim frame had started to sag under her new weight. Cyril was all for them having the baby; he made good money. He said, "Ultimately, it's your body, your choice. I will love and support you, no matter what". Preet decided that she just could not keep the baby. She was so sorry, so deeply sorry but there was just too much at stake. Plus, her mom had started to notice her weight gain and Preet was running out of excuses.

At four months, they decided that they had to get rid of the baby. Cyril hated that phrase "get rid of" as if his child were garbage but decided that of such is the nature of things, since we don't always have autonomy over our lives. They simply had to get an abortion that was the only option worth considering; even though, a year, even six months prior, this idea would have disgusted them but the current situation caused them to see this as a saviour (mostly Preet though). She figured that she could seek redemption after. Now she understood how a woman could make such a difficult decision to abort her child. A most painful reminder to not judge people without walking in their shoes.

Through the down town underbelly, Cyril found a doctor who agreed to do the procedure despite the fact that she was already in her second trimester. The doctor did caution them that it was late in the pregnancy and that they should be prepared for a number of eventualities which could include a hysterectomy. This, in and of itself was a scary thought but Preet felt like it would have been worth the risks involved for the sake of her parents' approval. Oh yes, the whole pregnancy thing had scared her into submission. She made promises to whichever gods would listen that she would be a good girl, break up with Cyril and go back to honouring her parents. She praised Jesus for His mercies and thanked Him for His faithfulness.

So, on a beautiful spring morning, there was a crisp wind, not too cold, birds were chirping and the new spring flowers had started to announce their arrival and intentions to hang around for a while. They both went to the basement apartment of a beautiful brick house, with well manicured lawns, red brick finish and a garden. This was the kind of house that dreams were made off. From the outside you could see huge glass windows and elegant tapestries. This house was set amongst lush green trees, hidden behind a metal fence. Yes, this was the backdrop to their bright future.

Cyril was not allowed to go in while the procedure was being done. He was visibly shaken and paced back and forth non-stop for the entire time; although, he had been assured by both Preet and the surgeon that everything would be fine. The surgeon told them that the procedure would be standard but he would spare them the details. Pretty much an in and out procedure and they would be on their way to start their new life.

Chapter 10

Cyril's Anguish – The Aftermath

After about an hour and a half, the practitioner came to inform me that Preet had not made it. Had not made it? What does that mean "had not made it"? This is another phrase that I have come to absolutely detest, to this day. What does it even mean? Had not made what? After that I zoned out. I didn't know what the heck I was expected to do now? I didn't even hear the explanation, something about the fetus being "bigger than anticipated". Again, more ambiguities, what does that mean? On top of that, the practitioner would not allow me to see her. He thought it best. He said he would handle the details because there was nothing that I could do for her anymore. I was going out of my mind and being a nervous wreck – I was not thinking clearly – I left the love of my life, with her life slowly ebbing from her forever, with only strangers to pick up the pieces.

This is definitely not a situation that happens every day: I was out of my depths – no frame of reference. For someone, more exposed, more mature than me, this might have been a walk in the park but for me, this was Herculean in nature. Compounded by the fact that, I didn't even know who to contact because our relationship was top secret so I didn't know any of her friends or family members, not even a distant cousin.

Lost and confused, I turned to my best friend – Austin – who convinced me to return to the doctor's office so that at the very least she could have a proper burial. We both went back; however, although I was quite certain of the address because I had Googled it and it was saved to my phone, the man who answered the door was a complete stranger, who said he had no idea about any physician living at that address. That was the last straw, I lost it because I knew for sure that I was not going crazy. The homeowner threatened to call the police and after a while we had to leave. What would we or what could we have said to the police? How could people just disappear? This wasn't the Twilight Zone! Heart broken, we left, not knowing what to do or what exactly had happened to Preet or who the doctor really was. So many questions and no answers were forthcoming. From that time, I came to abhor doctors.

I swore that I would never put anyone in that position ever again; hence, my vow to never, ever fall in love again. After all, love hurts. It wrenches out your heart, stumps all over it then puts it back in your chest and order you to put the pieces back together again. As a matter of cold fact, both Austin and I vowed to never speak of that day ever again. Everyone would call us crazy: for one, no one knew that I had been dating her, there was no body, no doctor; hence, no crime had been committed. We listened to every newscast, every news station, watched the news in the States, out West – to hear if a mysterious body had appeared – but nothing; *no dice* as aunt Felecie use to say. It was almost as if Preet never existed, she never lived and breathed and had dreams. After a while, even her phone stopped ringing.

For a long time, I was deeply anguished: I fell into a deep sadness and ultimately a great depression. I wore guilt like a second skin. I would take it off before going on stage to perform and then put it back on after the meet and greet. This is the type of depression, borne of repression, which might have crippled someone less resilient but definitely not me – son of Vince and the nephew of Felecie Parks. Ultimately, I found a way to make pain serve me by becoming the most famous and well-paid comedian in North America. I have frequent gigs all across Canada and I have performed in all fifty States, all across Europe, the Caribbean and the continent of Africa. All the time, wearing both guilt and pain; which was a weird thing, because while being crushed under the weight of their intensity; I still find a way to make people laugh: yes, sometimes they would laugh until they cried, I did as well, all the time knowing that I wasn't crying alone and I would never have to explain my tears.

Chapter 11

A Time to Mourn

My aunt's death has really shaken me to my core. I'm thinking about so many things that I have fought long and hard to bury. I'm feeling things that I can't even begin to describe because as vast as my vocabulary is, I have never been really big on emotions so this is quite new for me and quite scary. Yes, that's a perfect word – scary. I am so scared. I feel like my well-ordered existence is changing too rapidly without my permission. That's another thing, I've never been big on change! I like things the way I like things, just so: period! How dare aunt Felecie die and leave me in this emotional pickle! She left just when I needed her most.

My aunt has led such a complex life, most of which I had to force myself to acknowledge when I was writing her eulogy. As individuals we all need to be acknowledged for our contributions to humanity. That saying is really true that no one leaves planet Earth unscathed and really that slap after we leave the birth canal is a harbinger of many such pummelling to come.

The most surprising discovery I make is that most of my aunt's church family knew nothing of her mental health issues. They said they had never seen her exhibit any of the symptoms; only the contrary, they said Sister Parks was affable, always knew how to make everyone laugh. I guess we are more alike than I care to admit. We both laugh to keep from crying.

Now I am all alone in the world, no family, no true friends - well except for Austin. As a result of all this introspection and reflection, I realize that if I don't make some positive changes in my life I'm going to end up cold and alone. But when you've built walls around your heart for so long, you can actually forget how to get out from behind the walls you've built. Yes, I am a successful comedian right now but what will happen if or when they don't laugh anymore and instead of laughing with me they laugh at me? That's every comedian's worst nightmare.

It's not a new year or anything but I have made some resolutions in honour of my auntie. I have to find a way to honour her life in the way I choose to live mine. I need to figure out how to break free of my past. It's time to bury the past just like I buried my aunt. It was hella hard but it had to be done and I did it. I have to find a way to forgive myself for what happened to Preet. Sure, I have to take responsibility for the role I played in her untimely demise but ultimately, we both had a role to play. The question is: how can I move on without closure? Although I sometimes think that closure is overrated. But maybe that is to be my eternal punishment; to live with an overactive conscience and a very vivid imagination. I have imagined so many and various versions of this scenario sometimes I'm afraid to close my eyes.

I return to my house alone; my nest as Austin calls it. There are still things I need to sort out at my aunt's bungalow but that's tomorrow's job, today I don't have the energy. Tonight, I am exhausted: mentally, physically and emotionally. I make a peanut butter sandwich, aunt Felecie always use to make me this sandwich; I hated it, but today it's comfort food. God, I have so many questions. Auntie was always there, why didn't I just make the time to ask her. For instance, what's my mom's name? Not my dad's wife, my birth mom? How does she look? Is she pretty? Did she ever love me? Is she still alive? Where exactly does she live in Jamaica? Jamaica is not that big, I guess I could go looking for her! But where do I start? I finish my sandwich with a sigh. Maybe I should watch some tv to get my mind off these things. Maybe I'll get new material for my up coming gigs. How could I be the embodiment of success on the outside: the cars, the house, the millions, fame; yet, be such a failure on the inside? This is exactly what I did not want. I have never wanted to be a public success and a private failure. What's the point of success without contentment?

I must have dozed off because I was startled by the doorbell. I look through the peep hole and it's: sturdy and dependable Austin.

"Hey Austin!"

"Hey Cyril! How are you bud? I thought you could use some company!"

"Well, as usual, you thought right!"

"Here, I brought your favourite: jerk chicken, festival and coleslaw!"

"Thanks man, this is awesome!" I take the parcel from Austin; although, I'm really not hungry. But he's been considerate, I hate to say no. I'll just have some now and leave the rest for later.

We sit in the silence and let it wrap itself around us. That's the beauty of knowing someone since forever; not too many words are required. I'm actually touched by his gesture: no stupid questions, no questions that involve feeling words. At the church people kept asking me if I'm alright! Like really! Of course, I'm not ok! How could I be! My universe is coming unglued. I'm thankful for Austin, he too has remained constant and he never judges me. He's always in my corner. Come to think of it, he's more like the brother I never had.

Before you know it, the clock strikes twelve. Where does the time I go? Lately, I've been asking myself this question more often than I care to remember. Where does the time go? Are the minutes and hours collected somewhere, recycled then returned to us? Or maybe they are collected, stored and once they are spent, they expire forever. Sigh! So many questions and so very limited answers. Austin decides to stay over, and I can't say that I am not grateful.

I'm already dreading going to my aunt's house in the

morning but someone has to do it. It's the very least I can do for someone who has done so much for me: put *her* house in order. Hell, I need to put *my* house in order and I'm not talking about the nest.

Chapter 12

Cyril meets Zimera

I've never been one to believe in fate or coincidence. However, I do believe in spiritual connections based on energy patterns; which means that basically we are all connected by energy. On my way to my aunt's house, I kept feeling this vibe, like something was off. I know I'm ricocheting from a terrible trauma which has stirred other such traumas in me. Traumatic events that I have worked my whole adult life to suppress and here I am feeling a deep sense of regression. Do you know that feeling that you sometimes get but you can't explain it, you just can't put it into words? Intuitively, I feel like I'm about to be hit by a tsunami of emotions, just from being in her house.

I step onto auntie's porch, open the door and I had to do a double take to discern if I'm actually in the right house. Obviously, I am. I bought this house so absolutely I'm in the right house. There's a lady asleep on my aunt's couch – well – technically mine now. Someone

I've never seen before; come to think of it, she wasn't at the funeral. Although the state I was in, I doubt I would have noticed. She doesn't look familiar but she feels familiar.

Anyways, I clear my throat loudly twice and she is up with a start. I say, "Who the hell are you? Why the hell are you in my aunt's house?" To my surprise, she didn't even flinch. She yawned and stretched. I moved closer to her expecting her to speak but she just gawked at me. I assessed her as much as she was assessing me, as if she was trying to figure out if I am worthy. But worthy of what?

She is relatively short: about 5" 5", light brown complexion (just like me, Austin and auntie), she sports cornrows, I can see little wisps of silver mixed in with black hair and she has a mole on her right cheek. Mostly, I am drawn to her hands, she has very long elegant fingers; like a pianist, well manicured (not with nail polish but just well kept). In fact, she looks like she has never worked a day in her life. We appraise each other for a few minutes but in the way of awkward moments, it feels like hours.

At her leisure when she is good and ready, she declares, yes that's exactly what it is: a declaration! "I am Zimera!"

Zimera, Zimera! I taste the word! Where have I heard this word before. I try for a moment to call it to memory but I can't. I decide to let it go. When I'm not thinking about it, it will come back to me.

"I'm your aunt's friend and I got in late last night. But

I've not seen her all day. Where is she?"

I guess she saw the look on my face. Because she quickly adds, "She gave me a set of keys a while back!" I tried to delay the inevitable. I ask her, "Excuse me, but how do you know she's my aunt?" She points graceful, slender fingers at the mantle piece.

"OK! But I've never met you before! How do know my aunt?"

She nonchalantly says, as if talking to a child: "We've been friends since forever. And I've helped her out a few times when she was in great need".

Though the latter was said in a calm voice, it came with a conviction that said, *don't you even dare ask how I helped her.*

But I still had to say it because my ego was now on the line. "What do you mean, 'in need'?" "My aunt lacks, I mean lacked nothing!"

It was now her turn to make demands. "What do you mean 'lacked nothing'?" "Where is she?"

Still that calm, now almost soothing sound.

I don't know how to say it, neither do I want to put it out in the universe. It's too soon, too final. I had not accepted it yet, neither was I ready to accept it, the finality of it. The fact that my life is forever changed. But I couldn't lie to her. My damn conscience wouldn't let me. After all, they seemed to have been friends, she has a key and everything. I guess she is just another living, breathing example of how far I had drifted from my aunt. If they were that close, I should at least have known of her, right? Also, while it is easy to fool myself,

I couldn't, wouldn't deceive anyone else. That's just not my style. I try as best as possible to live with integrity. Fooling myself has become second nature; however, I wasn't about to share that with anyone, especially an obvious stranger.

I tell her that aunt Felecie had passed away the week prior of a suspected overdose. I refuse to accept that my aunt had committed suicide. Plus, the autopsy results were not back yet. I absolutely refuse to concede that my sweetly saved and sanctified aunt had put out her light.

Instantly, her calm demeanour changes. A complete metamorphosis: her eyes become orbs, her nose flares; she bore holes into me. She quickly composes herself and emphatically declares, "That is simply not true! She did not commit suicide! How could you of all persons believe that?" She says accusingly.

I am not about to explain myself to a complete stranger. I insist that she has to leave because I am just about to sort out my aunt's stuff and put the house on the market. She said she understands, but she was in town for the week and didn't have anywhere else to stay. I said, "Lady, with all due respect I don't even know you! For all I know you could be a stalker or worse, a serial killer."

Again, she doesn't even wince. She simply asserts, "She was my friend". This is said with so much conviction that I actually start believing her. She thinks for a moment and says, almost as if she had read my mind: "Tell you what, I know you don't really want to go through your aunt's stuff, so why don't I just do it for you! I'll put them in two piles: keepsakes and delete. Which will probably make it easier for you, if you want to get rid of more stuff."

I start to form a counter argument and she stops me before I speak.

"OK, how about I pay you to stay here for the week?"

This is so creepy; a complete stranger so desperately wants to stay in the house of a recently deceased person. I am about to say, absolutely not; plus, I don't even need *her* money. But for reasons, that I probably will never know; that's not what I verbalize. All I hear myself say is:

"OK, suit yourself. But one week and only one week. I don't need your money. And I *will* call the police if you go beyond that."

She extends her hand to shake mine but I decline. Another one of my idiosyncrasies: I hate to be touched by strangers.

In short order, she walks me to the door and I am on my way to my car. Suddenly, it dawns on me that she, this stranger, has successfully thrown me out of my own house. Like who is this woman? I also realize that I have not been given a surname name. She has a really unusual christian name that for some reason sounds quite familiar. It sounds like one of those medications being advertised on tv.

I call Austin to whine about this most bizarre encounter that I've had with a stranger who doesn't exactly feel like a stranger. I also tell him that I really don't know why I said yes. It goes against my nature to say yes to something like this: a stranger staying at my house, to say yes to a complete stranger. I've made it this far without a lawsuit and I don't intend to initiate one against myself. For all I know she could be a crazed fan. He laughs at this and says,

"Paranoid much are we! Or maybe, a little ego is getting in the way!"

I have no clue what he's talking about but I don't have enough energy to fight with both him and the weird lady, so I grudgingly let it go. Plus, he says something that makes sense. He says it must be the grief and possibly at a subliminal level, she reminds me of aunt Felecie. Trust Austin to psychoanalyze my situation. I tell him all the time that he is in the wrong field. He should be a shrink instead of a computer geek.

With a sigh, I say goodbye and hang up. Can this day possibly get anymore bizarre!

Also, I can't help but muse that Austin is definitely one of a kind. I shudder to think about how I would ever manage without him. He too has been bruised many times by traumas but seems to have become the better for it. Austin is one of the most empathetic persons I have ever met. I guess trauma; especially childhood traumas, make humans more aware of the human condition and more in touch with the emotions of others as they can recognize those emotions in themselves. I guess that is one of the reasons for the *emoji* generation. Somethings are easier expressed with an emoji.

Chapter 13

Austin's Torment

Austin Blane grew up with both his parents: Stacy and Fiona Blane. Yes, his dad's name is Stacy. His mom worked as a secretary at an Elementary school for years until she retired. She was always the voice of reason in their home and in his head. She was and still is the only constant in an ever-changing world. On the other hand, his dad is an entirely different story.

Both his parents migrated from Jamaica before he was born and the transition was very difficult for them; which is all part and parcel of the immigrant experience. No matter where you are from in the world, whether or not you are from a "shit hole country" the transition is never easy. Nothing ever really goes according to plan; especially, if you happen to be a member of a minority group, or if you identify as "other". There are already systemic issues entrenched in racist or discriminatory policies to force you either to leave or try to break you if you stay.

While his mom thrived in her new environment, his dad wilted and became increasingly more reserved, until he eventually became a shell of himself. He worked construction for many years and did quite well in the busy season. Clearly, his income was enough when matched with Fiona's to give them a comfortable lifestyle. Sadly, satisfactory was never enough for him. He was never enough. In retrospect, it's difficult to change negative ways of thinking especially when you enter a space where by your mere presence, the fact that you exist is not enough. There is always that subtle undertone and sometimes blaring to be more, give more, do more.

Stacy was never satisfied with his portion in life and felt powerless to change it. Like most men his age, he fell into the mental trap of thinking that his power was external. He thought validation from outside himself was paramount and he never acquired the courage to look within himself to find his true power, his core strength.

Like most immigrants, Stacy had big dreams and great expectations for himself and his family coming to Canada. Based on the fairy-tale, rose petal worldview he was sold by other immigrants, who weren't brave enough to share their struggles for fear of being judged. He thought that life would be a breeze. Also, he desperately missed his home and native land: the slow pace of life and the friendly, banter even among strangers. The older he got the more depressed and repressed he became but naturally being a man of few words lacked the words of emotional vulnerability to free his soul.

Needless to say, Stacy, like so many other men before him, who felt helpless against life's challenges; eventually, turned to alcohol which became his mistress, master, oppressor and best friend. The irony is that he had seen this happen to others and at the time swore up and down that it would never happen to him. Unfortunately, his situation provided the catalyst for the bottle to become his soul companion and while it destroyed him and his relationships: he felt like he had passed the point of no return and therefore felt that it was useless to resist its talons. Fiona often jests that the bottle was his "*side chick*".

That being said, their life was far from being humorous because Mr. Blane would frequently get home drunk and the words he lacked when sober would come spilling out of him like an avalanche. His soul had soured, so his words were bitter, which deeply scarred the young Austin and often left him perplexed and confused. Also, Austin became convinced that his dad hated him and it was his fault that his dad had become that way. After all, looking at the beautiful, smiling faces beaming from pictures on the wall; there was a time, before him, when they were happy, a time when no harsh words were never spoken, when smiles were served all around. Therefore, all the bitterness came with him. Yes, he was a package deal as he came with bitterness.

Naturally, Fiona was patient for a long time. Like most people of the female variety, she kept hoping and praying and wishing that he would change, that he would finally see the damage he was causing in their family and not to mention himself. But, no, he could not break free of his demons. Gradually, Fiona's main concern became her son. She watched him become angry while internalizing his father's behaviour and prayed that he would never become his dad. She prayed that he would have the mental fortitude and the courage to heal his soul so that he would never become his dad. She stayed throughout Austin's schooling and finally when he graduated from university, she had finally had enough so she divorced him. Not necessarily because she didn't need Stacy anymore because she loves him, will always love him but sometimes you have to come to the realization that you can not save anyone; no matter how much you love them. Sometimes leaving a toxic situation is more an act of self care than betrayal of vows.

Actually, the final straw came when Stacy showed up to Austin's graduation intoxicated and boisterous. That was just too much to bear. The divorce really angered Stacy because he seemed quite oblivious to the damage he caused. To be fair to Stacy, there's not an awful lot you remember when you spend most of your days and nights in a drunken stupor. Austin's astute sense of observation led him to this discovery but by then he had lost all regards for his dad. His dad had become the stranger who lived in their house and terrorized them on the regular. The stranger who caused his mom's silent tears, unspeakable sadness and decimated his childhood. By then it was just too much and everyone was just over the drama; except Stacy of course. Austin and Cyril often muse that parents initiate unspeakable damage in their child's life, then said child has to find the will to heal, then turn around and take care of the people who almost destroyed them and then the cycle would continue. They both vowed to never do that to anyone.

Over the years, both boys remained close friends, as Cyril was sometimes privy to Stacy's obstreperous outbursts and the only comment he would make is, "What do expect from a guy named Stacy?"

Invariably, they would laugh themselves senseless. Also, Cyril would never discuss anything that went on in Austin's world with anyone not even aunt Felecie. He somehow felt that they were part of the same tribe because in many ways, they had lived the same life. Cyril with his temperamental aunt and Austin with his constantly pickled dad. Yes, they occupied the same spheres of existence and became a lighthouse for each other.

Austin's mom managed to push pass the pain and had actually remarried; however, Austin seemed to have lost his bearings and couldn't find his way to love, to companionship. Fiona, naturally encouraged him by pointing out that: "Your father has made a choice to destroy his life! Please do not allow him to destroy yours in the process!"

Like any good son, he would say, "Sure mom, whatever you say!"

But in the recesses of his heart, he would grumble: *Too late! I'm already doomed.*

Intuitively, she seemed to understand those unspoken words. In fact, despite his young age, Austin felt like everything was too late for him. His mom frequently laughed at him, saying,

"Bwoy, yu old before yu young!"

Another one of her Jamaican proverbs, that only served to confuse him, as they made absolutely no sense to him. The other one that she loves to use is: "Austin, sometimes you have fe tek bad tings mek laugh!"

That one he understood because Cyril had explained it to him. It means, despite the many evils which plague your world, you have to take time out to laugh because laughter is a natural remedy that will not only heal the soul but is also a gatekeeper to protect the soul. This seems to be a part of the psyche of Jamaicans because they are always laughing – loudly. You can pretty much identify them anywhere and everywhere by that laughter which seems almost like a chorus for them.

Austin surmised that he had to hate his dad to love himself. He has actually verbalized this to Cyril. "I cannot allow myself to embrace him as my dad because then I would have to accept that there's a part of him in me. But which part: the abuser or the provider? No way could I or would I be able to do that either. Absolutely not after I had fought tooth and nail to get to this place on my journey where I can actually function; fought all my life to not become him. There was no way I'm going to mess that up by hanging around him either. Out of sight, out of mind, just the way I like it".

As Celina Gomez says so eloquently, *I have to hate him to love me. I have to lose him to find me.*

Chapter 14

Cyril's Time to Heal

I've had such an overwhelmingly busy day that I cannot sleep. I toss and turn for hours. I read, I watch TV, but sleep evades me. And that's the annoying thing because I have a sense that it is in the room, hovering around my bed, sometimes sitting at the foot of the bed, all the time, amused, yes greatly amused at my pain. I finally get out of bed and go downstairs to get a snack: milk and *bulla cake* (a Jamaican pastry that auntie use to buy from Caribbean stores). It's like a flat cake, which is generally hard; not rock hard, that's a different pastry called *donkey corn*. I don't exactly know if it's the milk or the *bulla* but whatever it is, it is working because I feel wonderfully drowsy, the precursor to sleep. I just let drowsiness take me away, like I'm floating on a cloud and I enjoy every moment of it. This great peace which surpasses my understanding. I think, this must be exactly how auntie felt before she took her last nap. That's deeply morbid but I just let my mind roam free. When you've been as tense as I have been, you enjoy every bit of freedom you can find.

In no time, I'm dreaming again, but it feels real. You know, one of those dreams where you feel like you want to pee and, in the dream, you go to the bathroom but only to wake up with your sheets wet. Yes, it feels real and familiar! It's one of my reoccurring dreams. Well, familiar is safe so I just go with the flow of the dream. To be frank, if it's a fighting dream, I'd prefer to just wake up and stay up all night because I don't have any energy to fight. I feel like all the fight is gone out of me.

I'm back at my aunt's old apartment, the tiny one (familiar grounds). I hear a weird sound and I realize that there is a monster in her house. There is always a monster but this time it is not the *Incredible Hulk* monster which it usually is (a big, bright green monster). It is a huge computer with flashing lights, like disco lights of all the colours of the rainbow. At first, I'm drawn to the colours, I'm mesmerized by all the colours, but then I realize that the monster computer is coming after me while making indistinguishable sounds. I think, *oh man, this thing is really going to make me run! I can't catch a break, not even in my own dreams. In my own dreams, in the warmth and comfort of my own bed and in the refuge of my own mind, I'm being bullied! No where is safe for me anymore.*

Anyways, I start to run but, I become aware of a new twist to this dream; usually and by usually, I mean, every single time I've had this dream (which is often) I run away from the apartment; however, some how I always end up right back there, right back where I started. Right back where most of my childhood traumas happened. The new twist is that, I actually run away and stay gone. I don't end up anywhere near that apartment. I'm literally so relieved, I could cry. I've finally escaped the monster in my dream which has terrorized me my entire adult life.

The next morning, I wake up with a smile on my face. My first real smile in how many years. I feel like this dream is an omen; letting me know that my life is about change for the better, that I'll be embarking on a new adventure, a new journey. I hope and pray that this will be a pleasant journey. I definitely have had my fair share of bad luck. So much so, that sometimes I feel like I am paying debts that I didn't owe. I am done trying to convince myself that *to whom much is given, much is required.* How come I've only inherited pure and unadulterated pain? When will it be my turn to reap some good karma? When am I going to reap the pleasant fruits of my labour? When is it going to be my turn?

I must admit, I do feel groggy from all the running in my dream; plus, being up most of the night, but I feel inspired as well. You know that feeling you get when the sun is shining in the Spring, the birds are chirping, when random strangers smile at you in the streets and you smile too despite yourself, because everything is beautiful. Also, there's a new freshness to life, like a new beginning, like anything could happen, like you could actually win this round of the fight.

The feeling of forlorn and alarm and being excessively vigilant has lifted and I feel like I want to drink up everything that life has to offer. I shower quickly to get the residue of sleep out of my eyes. I decide to have a nice sit-down breakfast at Tim Hortons. On my way, I call Austin to see if he wants to meet up but he's already at the office so we make plans to meet up later.

After breakfast, I pay a visit to my aunt's house to see how Zimera or Zumera (I can't remember her name clearly) is doing with the packing. When I get there, I realize that she has accomplished a lot. She already has boxes of junk waiting at the curb. When did my aunt become such a hoarder? One of the many questions I would have loved to ask her.

I knock on the door, forgetting that I too have a key. I was reaching for it when she answered the door. We exchange pleasantries about the spring weather then she says, "I don't think we started off on the right foot yesterday. I apologize for not being more sympathetic towards you. I was in a state of shock myself. So, I just want us to start afresh today".

"Ok, that's cool".

"Hi, my name is Zimera. Nice to meet you and thank you so much for your hospitality". Zimera doesn't extend her hand this time.

I guess as a peace offering she offers me tea but I decline on account of the huge breakfast that I just devoured. She says while she was clearing out stuff, she found old photo albums that she thinks I should have. Yes, those are her exact words "you should have!" Well of course, this is my house. This woman is so, so, so, I search for the word – pushy! Not the right word but I know it will come to me. I'm really good with words but she is really testing my patience… not quite jarring on my nerves yet but she's getting there.

Anyways, the first album contains mostly my pictures. I am kind of surprised because I didn't know auntie had so many pictures of me from when I was a baby until around the age I left home. The next looks like a scrapbook. She has newspaper clippings of my life as a comedian, even a few articles from two of Canada's top magazines: *Maclean's* and *Chatelaine* about my journey. I'm so deeply moved by the gesture; I fight back tears. This is what happens when I remove my defences: tears. All my life, I've worked hard keeping my defences up, my shield ready but in an unguarded moment, tears threaten to weaken my resolve. Not just regular tears but the deluge which I have always feared.

I analyze each image page by page evaluating my evolution. I am drawn to an image of me playing in the sand with a ginormous smile on my face. I seem so carefree and yes, happy. This was when I was really young and we had returned to Jamaica, for someone's funeral. I know it was definitely a funeral because that's the sole event that would demand that my aunt "sacrifice" to go. That's always a strange concept for me, I always wonder: why spend so much money to attend the funeral of someone you've not spoken with in years, or someone you don't even like? I guess that was her way of making sure that they were really dead and it wasn't just a rumour.

I am awe struck by the surroundings in the picture,

I feel a sense of nostalgia. The sand, the sea, people in the sea and walking on the shore, in varying states of undress, all the smiling faces; people who seem so relaxed, so at peace with themselves and who seem so entirely certain of their purpose in life. I wonder how my life would have turned out if I had grown up in Jamaica. This is just a passing fancy because I know from first hand experience that there is absolutely no going back to change the past; absolutely no do-overs. Plus, I have resolved to put the past behind me: let the past be just that, the past and live in the moment.

This whole day, no from the dream; to everything else which has unfolded, has me feeling disheveled. I can hardly maintain my composure. Oh man!

Zimera, clears her throat, bringing me back to the present, but that image is forever burnt into my memory. I'll carry that image with me to remind myself that there was a time when I was happy and somewhere out there, out in the world, there are happy people and maybe one day, just maybe one day, if all the stars line up in my favour, I will be able to find happiness as well. For me, happiness has become a destination, a place of rest where I can safely unpack and salvage what can be salvaged of my half-baked life.

I force myself back to the present, which is the other thing on my to do list: live in the moment. She brings me yet another album. This one houses pictures of me and my family members. I see my dad, his wife and of course aunt Felecie with my grand parents. What exactly is Zimera trying to do to me? Aunt Felecie is in most of the pictures with me, she has been ubiquitous to my existence for a really long time. I am really going to miss her. I only hope that she knew how much I loved and appreciated all she did for me and that I am eternally grateful for all the sacrifices she made. I'm struck by the fact that, no where in this album is a boyfriend or even a girlfriend, no significant other: she always kept her arms open so that she could hold me at anytime. At least I had Preet for a moment in time and still have Austin. There I go again, regurgitating things, I vowed to never think of again.

It is all too intense for my frayed nerves, I capitulate to the tears. I let them subjugate me, seeking relief from their oppression, oh wicked tears.

Zimera is intuitive enough to give me privacy, for that I am grateful. After all, she is still a stranger.

I'm not even going to front, I really needed this moment. I needed to have one last cry. And looking at these pictures is somehow the wake that I needed to experience solace.

I experience all five stages of grief in less than an hour. Now that my tears are spent, I resolve that from this moment on: I will live life to the fullest, without regret. I suddenly realize that I've never truly lived as I have spent most of my life stuck at twenty, the age when I made the worst mistake of my life.

Again, I feel the deluge of tears gushing from me and I feel like they will never end. However, these tears are cathartic and they needed to be spent. God gave us all tear ducts for a reason; both men and women. Women don't own the rights to tear duct cleaning. It is as much a man's right to tears as it is a woman's. Again, I resolve to give myself permission to cry whenever there's a need. At this, I literally feel a weight leave my shoulders. I feel all the sadness leaving me and I decide to embrace just the lessons that remain.

It is amazing how a single moment can change a life, stir a change in direction. A few days ago, I faced one of the worst days of my life and here I am today, with a renewed sense of hope and a new zest for life. It is as if, I've suddenly found the elixir of life, the one most fitting and appropriate for *my* life. All these years, I've been afraid to cry because *a man is not supposed to cry*, wasted years. Zimera has come to sit next to me, she doesn't speak, she allows me to have my moment and it doesn't feel weird anymore, me crying in front of a stranger.

Gradually, I take charge of the situation and thank her for decluttering my aunt's house. She says it's her pleasure to help Felecie one last time.

I am about to leave but, on an impulse, carried away by my emotional release, I invite her to my house for dinner. At first, she says she doesn't want to inconvenience me but then there's a look of empathy in her eyes and she accepts. I leave excited to buy groceries to cook for her and Austin. I have not cooked for anyone, not even myself, in ages.

On the drive home, while reflecting on the day I've had, I can't help but once again muse on how familiar Zimera feels. Honestly, she genuinely feels like one of my reoccurring dreams. Being around her feels like being around family. I rationalize that auntie has told her a lot about us, about me, so that makes her feel close somehow. I know for sure that she couldn't be related to me: no disrespect to my ancestors but she seems way too normal, too in control of herself. She stirs a desire in me to want to heal, to be whole. It's like the universe is saying, *you've been messed up all your life son, here is an example of what normal looks like, what healed feels like so you can go forth and emulate this example.* I laugh at the image in my head of the sky, using a fluffy cloud to point to Zimera.

But really, what does it really mean to be healthy, to be healed? This is not a concept I've allowed myself to get familiar with.

The phone rings and disrupts my reverie. I see from the call display that it's Austin. "Hey dude! How are you?"

"Taking a rough life soft, as my mom use to say!"

I laugh because that is so Jamaican. I invite him to dinner and tell him about Zimera. He mischievously questions: "Dude, who is this woman? Is she a devil or an angel? Because she seems to have you under a spell!"

"And what exactly makes you say that?" I say this teasingly.

"Bro you NEVER cook!"

We both *dead wid laugh* (the Jamaican version of LOL) at his candour because we know it's true. I tell him that I am not quite sure myself *who or what* she is but he could decide that for himself later. He said, "OK, I'll be there with bells on!"

I'm like, "What does that even mean!"
He says, "You've never heard that before?"
"NOPE!"
"It means I'm excited to attend your little party if for no other reason than to meet Zimera!"

We bid farewell and I race home to make my own version of curried chicken, white rice and coleslaw. Later, I will have to issue a disclaimer that it is my own unique touch so it might not turn out the way they are accustomed but for sure, no one will die. Hopefully.

Chapter 15

A Time to Pluck up That which has been Planted

Austin

I hang up from Cyril feeling elated. I can't remember the last time he's been in such good spirits. His joy is infectious because I suddenly have a smile on my face. When you've been friends with someone for as long as we have; it's easy to tell their mental state, even over the phone.

My mind goes back to a time when Cyril was this happy, it was my thirteenth birthday and my mom had planned a birthday party. It was something like a *bar mitzvah* because my mom said it was to signify that I'm on my way to becoming a man. It was just me, Cyril and three of my friends but it was magic.

My birthday is in June so it wasn't freezing but it wasn't that hot either. The weather seemed to reflect my place in the world; not yet a man but definitely not still a boy.

A period in my life which in retrospect, I refer to as *an in between place.*

My mom set up a small tent in the tiny backyard and she had the barbecue going. We had hotdog, burgers, jerk chicken and jerk pork. Along with all that came the biggest birthday cake I've ever seen. We played a variety of games: card games, marble, tag and my Indian friend Paviter, introduced us to *Four Corners*. We played this game on the street in front of my house and other kids joined in. *Four Corners* as the name suggests is literally choosing four central spots and someone is chosen as *it*. The rest of us have to swap spots without being touched by *it*. It was lots of fun but Paviter always won so we quit playing after a few rounds.

After that it was time to cut the cake and I asked my mom if all my friends could have a slice and she said yes, as long as it was ok with their parents. Pretty soon, our tiny backyard was filled with boys, of varying colours, ages and sizes. Every time I look back at that day, I understand why some philosophers believe that there is absolutely no scientific evidence for race and that race is just a social construct. Simply because that evening there was no white boy, black boy or brown boy, it was a group of boys playing in our backyard, just having fun. In that group, there was no "other" because none was excluded. To this day, whenever I'm in a group setting, I always look for the commonalities, the threads that unite us rather than the things that separate us.

It was an amazing day. I still smile when I reflect on my thirteenth birthday. However, it was bittersweet because that same night, my dad broke my arm and sent me to the hospital. It's weird how a small thing can escalate into something way bigger. Something that's beyond our human comprehension, our ability to process. Dad came home drunk as usual and started yelling at mom. Apparently, she had reprimanded him for missing my party and it went on for hours. By then, I had gotten tired of him belittling and berating her. I stood between them and that's when he put me in a choke hold and twisted my hand behind my back. I heard a crunching sound and knew instantly that I wouldn't be using my right hand for a while. My mom managed to get him off of me and rushed me to the hospital. All the way there, I begged her to report him to the police but she refused. For the life of me, I couldn't understand why. After all, this is Canada and isn't the law on the side of the weak? Also, she made me lie to the doctor and nurses that I fell off my bike. I didn't even have a bike at the time. Up to this day, I'm still angry at her because after that incident the abuse just got progressively worse for both of us because obviously he knew he would get away with it.

Eventually, she divorced him but that was way after the damage had been done to both us. To this day, I still resent my mom because that night could have changed the trajectory of our lives forever. Every time I asked her why she stayed, she said it was complicated. Not to me though! He's a jerk so you leave him. The End! Period! Why do we always try to place a comma where a period should be?

I guess the seeds of resentment run so deeply for my

mom that I never even considered getting married. It's funny how one seed of resentment yields so many other negative fruits: bitterness, malice, unforgiveness, and the list goes on. I'm not going to lie; I've been so bitter towards mom that I hardly call her. I didn't even attend her wedding. I'm just so over the BS. I just want to live, my own life and forget about my parents and their dysfunction. They made me become this subpar version of myself and I've been this way for so long that I don't even know how to find my way back to myself.

Chapter 16

Zimera: A Time to live

There is a deep cry of the soul which brought me to Cyril, not his call but his aunt Felecie's. Felecie whom I've helped before but only in a minuscule way because she was way too guarded. She always had her guard up; as a result of, unspeakable pain inflicted by her own family. In my line of work, those are generally the most difficult humans to help; those deeply impacted by familiar or romantic relationships. It was Felecie's guttural cries for Cyril that broke through the generational curse of poverty in his lineage. However, now there's a greater death coming to him: his soul is about to die. You see, when you've known the pain of disappointment and rejection your whole life, the part of the soul responsible for fighting for your survival everyday, gets really tired. Soon, it begins to shutdown. Most people don't know that the pain of loss is the most crippling because to counter the pain, the individual often reaches into his soul and try to scour the place where the loved one use to dwell. In the spirit realm we call this *Haifuwa* which literally *means to cleanse or sterilize*.

It is now Cyril's time to live again, to not just merely exist but to live to his fullest potential and to become his best self. How the world works is that people depend on each other for the inspiration or energy to fulfill their potential so, when someone is not at their post (place of awakening) those depending on him are impacted and might die without ever attaining their full potential. They might even take longer to attain self actualization just because the one responsible to deliver their inspiration is not at his post. This creates a ripple effect because other souls are waiting on their epiphany or awakening as well. For instance, have you ever met someone or know of someone (maybe a public figure) who triggers a desire in you to live (not just barely survive), to be creative, to activate your potential: well that person was in his spot or place at the right time, to trigger that response in you. Cyril's job as a comedian is not just to make people laugh, but to inspire them and get them to think (put things in perspective).

Cyril has accomplished a lot in a short time but there are still dreams and aspirations left for him to accomplish. Cyril, I awaken in you the will to live, the will to heal and once you are healed your gift of laughter will heal others because it will never come from a place of bitterness but it will come from a place of hope and faith.

All that Cyril has gone through is part and parcel of a process to build character in him. He can not fail at this point because failure is not an option or else he's going to have to keep going through similar struggles until he learns the lesson. I don't know if he's strong enough to keep doing that.

The absolutely saddest thing ever, is a comedian who only knows how to make others laugh from the core but he himself is broken to his core.

Chapter 17

The Fight

Cyril

It is amazing how what starts out as a beautiful day soon turns sour. All of a sudden, I wasn't happy anymore. I started to feel like a dark cloud was hanging above me and at any moment, it could spue sulphuric acid all over me. Aunt Felecie use to say that *"you can not trust your feelings"* but what other option is there? I did not want to have company anymore. How could I cancel at this point? What would I say? Austin and Zimera should be on their way by now. Plus, the meal is almost ready, what would I do with all this food? One thing I learned while growing up is never to waste food.

I do what I sometimes do to fight this deep foreboding of the soul: I turn to my little black book – my book of jokes. Which joke would suit my present situation? There is none. I have to write one and trust me, a *knock knock joke* will not work either. So where do I turn for inspiration? Believe it or not; the news. I turn to news stations for material because they are a constant, they might not always be consistently credible but they are a constant. Also, the familiarity of the news anchors and the key players (both public figures and regular people) is definitely comforting in a really weird way. As humans we all contribute to the stability of other humans; *each one teaching one,* as aunt Felecie use to say.

Before I could unpack my feelings, the doorbell rings and it's Austin. He looks more bummed out than I feel.

Zimera

I leave Felecie's house and make my way over to Cyril, by teleportation. I could have gotten there by flying but I feel a disturbance in the atmosphere. Even before I get there, I know that there will be a fight. I am ready! After all, this is the reason I came - to fight! I am here for it.

The first thing that catches my attention is a wall of *iidemons* (demons) lined up around Cyril's house. They form a ring around it as if to keep Cyril boxed in and me out; almost like a nest around him. I don't know how he has been able to survive in that house when he is surrounded by a huge *umkhosi* (army). The *iidemons* are all dressed in black, on black *karafa* (stallions) although *their* colours are as many and varied as the rainbow. They appear vicious and menacing but beautiful at the same time. Instinctively, I know who they are: the spirits of fear and loathing that come through bloodlines.

To counter their hate, I need to spread love (most people don't know this, but love is a very powerful magic). I choose the most fitting and appropriate weapon from my arsenal. I pick a *multi-bladed throwing knife*. I choose this weapon because it is deadly and once released it moves quickly in a circular motion, stabbing its mark. Over the years, I have come to realize that once released, some weapons take on a life of their own. This is one such weapon. Back in the day, these were used by the most aggressive Zulu warriors. I sprinkle love all over it and throw it at the epicentre of their band. There is a spark and a huge fire erupts, burning through their ranks. Some of the fringe soldiers see me and attack from all directions. They use tiny, fiery darts which are deceptive because they are tiny yet deadly. They burn through layers of skin in seconds; take it from one who has been burnt many times. These are considered *fear-mongers*. The ones who instill fear in the hearts of humans. I have to think quickly. I look for the tallest building in the area. I perch strategically to get an aerial advantage, so I can pick them off with my arrow one by one. That seems to slow them down but only temporarily. Now that many of them have been *teku (*seared by love*)* they are enraged so they look for the source of the attack.

They start to make high pitched, screeching sounds. I don't know what that means but soon enough I see streaks of green and red: I recognize right away that, that was their war cry – they are calling for reinforcement. These are the most deceptive and deadly spirits; spirits of envy and hate. The type of envy which prevents people from recognizing all they have gained because they are too busy looking at what their neighbours have. This can cause serious separation and *a dada* - in fighting - in families. This level of envy, almost always leads to hate and hate always leads to murder: not a physical death but the type which assassinates character.

I need reinforcements myself! There are literally too many of them for me to fight. This is usually where I fail because I generally wait too long to call for back up, NOT TODAY. I set off my flare arrow and soon enough, other ancestral spirits start to join me in the fight. All of them come equipped for the fight. We are all at once majestic and beautiful. Immediately, there are arrows of love, joy and peace being dispatched everywhere. The arrows take on a life of their own. At first, there's a shimmer, then a sparkle and soon there's a kaleidoscope of colours. We all pause to admire our handiwork. As the colours splash all over these spirits like rose petals, their defence systems start to weaken. One by one, they disappear, giving off a popping sound every time like the explosive sound of fireworks.

At last, it is just us left lingering over the scene like CSIs at a crime scene.

As if on cue, we hear anguished voices coming from the north, south, east and west: time for my back up to go on various missions wherever these anguished voices are located. My army take its leave and soon it is just me again: one solitary dove.

This battle seems to have raged forever but it was just about half an hour. Time is obviously different in the spirit realm. Thankfully, I won't be too late for Cyril's dinner. In my human form, by the time I get to the door I'm exhausted. I just want to take a nap but of course I can't because the fight was just the beginning; there is still lots to be done. Fighting the spirits was the easy part, now I have to convince a human with his own freewill to give up habits that he spent a lifetime creating. The more I think about it, is the more I want to go to bed. However, time is of the essence and I need to strategically strike while the proverbial iron is still hot.

Austin

It takes me such a long time to get to Cyril's house. As soon as I decide to leave work, everything that could go wrong did. I almost went straight home but Cyril seemed to have been in such great spirits this morning that I wanted desperately to share in his good fortune. By the time I leave work, it is rush hour and there has been a collision. This leads to a chain reaction pile up on the 401 which I didn't know of until I got on the ramp, then it was too late to do anything. I really should have just gone straight home eh. On top of that, the weather has turned sour as well. At first it is just rain, with lightning and thunder then it starts to hail. For literally thirty minutes it hails nonstop. I was mortified that my car would be damaged. I suddenly envy Cyril because he sets his own hours and works at his own pace.

Then just as suddenly as it started, the hail stops, the skies clear and there is even a bit of sunshine and a pale rainbow – only in Canada these other worldly weather patterns occur – without much warning sometimes.

Needless to say, by the time I get to Cyril's nest, I need a drink of the strongest kind.

Chapter 18

My Dinner Party

Cyril

Once we sit down to dinner, I feel a sense of calm come into my world. It must be the wine. Thank goodness for alcohol. At first, we are quiet but then we start exchanging sounds:

"Yummy!"

"Hhhhmmmmm!"

My guests actually love my cooking and their compliments make it worth all the effort. So happy I did not cancel. Even Austin is visibly more relaxed than I've seen him in a while. Zimera seems to have a very calming influence on people.

After dinner, we go to the living room with our dessert, where I intend to find out more about Zimera; especially, when and where she met my aunt and how they came to be friends.

Not to appear too brazen (as my aunt used to say). She believed that anyone who shows any sign of being assertive is "too much or *too dry eye*". I slowly build up to that question.

"Where are you from Zimera? What's your background?"

I find that, this is the most common question asked in North America. Because Canada is home to so many ethnicities, this is usually a fairly typical question. Almost everyone here (apart from the Native Indians) has an origin story that started somewhere else.

She thinks for a while. Which is also common because some people embody multiple ethnic identities. For instance, someone might be of Middle Eastern descent but was born in the UK, lived in the US for a while, before migrating to Canada. Also, when I was in high school, my grade twelve Social Studies teacher was big on embracing differences; therefore, she wanted to make a point about intersectionalities. She framed her discussion by beginning with the statement: *all the brown people stand at the door.* Of course, all the people of middle eastern descent headed for the door. At first, I was confused. I wasn't sure if I should go because, at the time, I thought that I was just a Black boy from Jamaica but a lot of people referred to me as being brown or "light skin". Eventually, she cleared it up for us by saying that typically most people embody different identities and that is quite fine. From that day, she literally gave me permission to be my "whole self" as she called it. To embrace all aspects of my identity, occupy my place.

Zimera begins, "I am originally from Southern Africa, my origin story begins with the Zulus. They go as far back as the seventeenth century".

Southern Africa is quite vague because that could mean, anywhere from: Angola, Namibia, South Africa to Zimbabwe. Literally from A to Z. Clearly, she is not in the mood to tell, so I let it slide. We might of necessity return to it later or at some other point.

But Austin states, "Zimera is a very unusual name. It is lovely though. What is your surname Zimera?"

She quickly states, "Wanda! A traditional Zulu clan name".

I guess she is eager to change the subject, as she questions:

"So, you must be wondering how I came to know your aunt?"

She asks before I could formulate my next question. Reading my mind, again. I answer in the affirmative.

"I met her at a time when she was going through a really difficult time. And then we met a few other times just to get caught up".

Austin questions, "If you don't mind me asking, what are some of the things that you ladies talked about?"

Zimera thinks for a moment and explains,

"Austin, while I won't be able to reveal specific details, we did talk generally about her childhood. In doing so, we discussed childhood traumas OR what is commonly known as *Inter Generational Traumas* or *IGTs.*"

Austin and I simultaneously ask:

"What?"

"It's generally a school of thought which postulates that trauma can be passed on from generation to generation".

It is my turn to interject: "You mean like a curse? Because I've heard my aunt talk about generational curse. She was always going on about it."

In the matter of fact tone that I am getting use to,

"It depends on who you ask. For in stance, some church folk will say they are the same; while non-church folks will say they are different".

Austin quizzes, "What do you say?"

"I believe that traumas sometimes happen for different reasons. Traumas are as diverse as family dynamics. There is no one way of defining them. They happen in rich families, poor families, black, white, pink, yellow families. A trauma can range from verbal abuse to physical, sexual and emotional abuse. So, in terms of trauma being a curse, if by curse you mean cycle or pattern, then yes. Outside of that context, I don't know if trauma is considered a curse or not. Also, in every family, there are ways of knowing and specific ways of doing things which is emulated and passed down from generation to generation. For example, ways of cooking and beliefs around religion."

"That's quite interesting! I know for sure that my aunt had a hard time growing up. But exactly what happened, I couldn't say. We never discussed those things. Even in terms of, sicknesses and diseases in our bloodline, we never talked about those".

"That's true in my family as well", Austin declares.

I watch Austin closely and he seems intrigued by this whole notion of IGTs.

Zimera asks, "What do you mean?"

"Well, my dad was sometimes abusive to my mom and I often wonder if that misogyny was a learned behaviour. Because everything would be fine, then something simple would happen and then he would snap. He would almost become a different person. I also use to wonder if he just lacked the skills necessary to deal with problems why he would turn to violence".

Zimera thinks for a moment and she looks as if she is looking for the perfect word or the most appropriate scenario to explain herself. I start to like her more and more; especially, because she is so welcoming to Austin and for the first time I really look at her. She is not really someone, one would call beautiful, in the traditional sense but she is beautiful in the way she emits warmth. I have heard people say, *he or she feels like home*. That's exactly what Zimera feels like – home sweet home. Which is quite ironic because my home growing up was anything but sweet. Sure, aunt Felecie and I had great moments. But generally, not that many. There was often confusion, periods of extreme silence or the other end of the spectrum lots of yelling. Also, as much as I loved my aunt, I can't actually say that I really knew her, like know her essence. After all, isn't that how we are supposed to know the people we love? Hearing all this although quite vague, confirms to me that she never had a great childhood. Which makes me feel really sad for my precious aunt.

Austin clears his throat and says, "How do we overcome this trauma? What would you recommend to a person who has suffered the effects of long-term trauma?"

He is really on a roll tonight.

Again, that intense look appears in her eyes and she looks like she is reaching into herself to pull out the right remedy. She begins,

"Well......"

Then more confidently, "It may seem like this is a very complex issue, which it is. Thus, the answer is often found in simple practices".

"You mean like yoga? Because I'm not doing that! I am a comedian and laughter is my medicine of choice!"

She smiles at me, "Cyril, yes indeed laughter is indeed the best medicine. But sometimes, people use things like laughter and church attendance to numb their pain. And don't get me wrong, I am not negating the importance of attending your local assembly or the positive impact of humour but those things are often used to numb pain instead of treating it. Because we all know that pain is pain; emotional, physical, it is all pain and it is generally the body's way of signaling for help".

Zimera

I notice that look in Austin's eyes, like he is on the verge of an epiphany. Apparently, *he* is comprehending what I am saying not only with his head but with his heart and soul as well. I am grateful that at least he's getting it. At that last comment, despite my attempts at caution, Cyril becomes overtly resistant; even his posture is resistant. Cyril's arms are placed across his chest;

almost as if, he feels the need to protect his vital organs from an intruder. This behaviour is textbook.

This often happens in individuals who have endured many traumas so, they build a wall, wall for their protection. Also, these individuals will enter relationships with these walls up, their partners find it difficult to connect with them emotionally because they have barricaded themselves inside and are unable to get out or let anyone in. They become emotionally unavailable. These individuals sometimes want to reach out, want desperately to get out but they have completely forgotten how - almost as if they have lost their key. Invariably, they are trapped in their own cycle of negative emotions, that feed into negative experiences, which manifests in toxic relationships. It is almost like Murphy's Law, in that, people are drawn to things that they fear or hate. This is why, seemingly logical women will end up in abusive relationships, with partners who in some way, reflect their fathers.

I decide to take a different approach with Cyril; apparently, I have triggered his natural defence mechanism.

Cyril

While I really like Zimera and her deep sense of empathy, I suddenly did not like the direction this conversation has taken. How could she assume that my art form that I have spent many years crafting is useless? Well, if I accept that mode of thinking, then it would suggest that I *am* useless or inadequate. I fought for years trying to hold on to this important part of me; to make people laugh, even when I didn't feel like laughing, so there is no way in hell I am letting this lady, this stranger, minimize my life's work. I try to not look directly at her but I feel powerless to resist her gaze. There is a kind of potent energy emanating from her which is captivating and Austin seems just as captivated as I am, even more so. Suddenly, there's a thought in my head – a mere suggestion, but it fills my consciousness, one word: FORGIVE.

This idea is a quiet presence in me. I find myself mouthing the word a few times. Zimera's face lights up and she exclaims,

"That is absolutely the correct answer, forgiveness is key!"

She says this like I had won some kind of contest, providing the correct answer before the buzzer sounds.

"But I've already made peace with my family members: my aunt, my dad and even my biological mom, although I've never met her!"

"That's wonderful!"

She says this while simultaneously bringing her hands together; as if to applaud my efforts, similar to an action I've seen aunt Fiona do many times.

"But while it's important that you're able to forgive others, it is also imperative that you are able to forgive yourself as well. Because often it is self loathing which insinuates these negative cycles. It is not as if these individuals go looking for an abuser but their energy and sometimes words are uttered in ignorance, sometimes even jest, which invites the wrong person in their space".

Austin declares, "That makes so much sense to me, now that I reflect on my parents' relationship. My mom always says, *"poor me"*. So maybe that's why my dad treated her poorly!"

Zimera replies, "That's overly simplistic but yes that's the general concept".

Austin really seems engrossed in this BS. He seems to have bought into it: hook, line and sinker. But not me! I see the kind of bull she's selling and I'm not buying it, at all. First of all, that is not a logical perspective. It's almost as if, she is equating trauma with genes which can be inherited from either parent. But in this case, we get to pick which ones and because of conditioning we choose the "negative" ones. Oh, gimme a break!

Zimera

Both boys are fiercely intelligent and quite insightful. I have really enjoyed our discussion; however, it is far more than apparent that I have lost Cyril. He has completely shut down. I can't even hold his gaze anymore and since I cannot tamper with free will there is absolutely nothing that I can do to regain his attention or his trust. This intervention is certainly not going as well as I had hoped. On the other hand, Austin is more accessible, more open, so I focus on him. Hoping that I have planted a seed in Cyril that Austin will nurture. I have always maintained that there is nothing conclusive in this world. Nothing is ever just black or white; there is always even a speck of grey or blue or pink and that is where most disagreements originate. Everything has subtle nuances and rightly so because it is all these complexities which account for the beauty in the world and also the brilliance which is humanity.

Thankfully, because there is already an opening in Austin's soul I am able to send what I call *ibhalsam* or balm for his soul which will initiate the healing process. This will help him to change his perspective because most certainly healing is all about perspective. And while healing is a process which can be messy, perspective is required to focus on what is required to complete this undertaking. This undertaking will not be accomplished overnight but with persistent and consistent effort healing can and will take place. The single most difficult piece of this conundrum is for an individual to admit and accept that he needs to heal.

It is time to go so I thank Cyril for the meal, and both of them for their company. I am quite disappointed that I am unable to reach both of them; however, I am confident that they will be fine. Afterall, they have each other for support so that's encouraging. Some people just take longer to find their way but most people do. Austin offers me a ride and I reluctantly accept because I am even more drained than before dinner. I was just hoping to step outside and disappear. But it is late and I don't wish to set off any alarms by insisting; because really how would I explain my mode of transportation to them, at this time of night, in this quite exclusive neighbourhood.

Chapter 19

Austin's Resolve

After, leaving Cyril's house I drop home Zimera, well I leave her at aunt Felecie's house. We drove in silence for the most part because she had given me so much to think about at dinner. It's amazing how life works sometimes, how you can meet someone for the first time, just once and they have a monumental impact on your life. Imagine how I've met her for the first time and the last as she leaves in a few days and she thoroughly gets me like no one else has. Imagine that! She sees through all my veneer. We all live in a world of illusions: some we have created while others were created for us. I guess some amount of fantasy is healthy but not so much that you lose yourself; lose your purpose. Most of us seem to live in a state of ambivalence which seems to rob us of our authenticity; to the point where, when people are genuinely honest, they are suspect. They are considered "pretentious" because they display a quality that seems to be drifting away from the human experience.

Also, they remind us of what we lack, what we have lost. Quite frankly, we look to others for validation because we don't know ourselves enough; therefore, we look to others and ask the question: who am I? We look to people who don't have a clue who they are to explain to us who we are.

As I leave auntie's house, I see Zimera in my rear-view mirror and she is the very epitome of peace. The type of peace that is so tranquil, it has an inherent infectious appeal. I have so many questions about her: where is she from? What is the source of her peace? While she sat in the passenger seat, with peace emanating from her, I wanted to ask her so many questions. However, I said nothing, not wanting to disturb the moment. Because this entire experience is a whole moment. A moment when time stood still and we got a chance to question our mortality. Sometimes in a quest to discover more, we miss a moment. So, I remain resolutely quiet and just soak up the moment.

After I bid her farewell, I am aware that I will never see her again. I am grateful to have been in her presence for even a nanosecond because she has completely transformed my worldview. Suddenly, the world doesn't seem as menacing as it did before. As I watch her glide to aunt Felecie's door, again I am struck not only by the fluidity of her movements but how utterly certain she is of her destination. Each step to her door propels *me* closer to my fate.

My heart swells with familial love for her – for a stranger. I almost laugh at the lunacy of the notion because yes, I have never met her prior to tonight; however, she feels like my tribe. I depress the gas pedal and I know exactly what my next move will be.

"Siri call mom!"

Immediately she picks up, almost as if she's been waiting for my call.

"Hi baby!"

"Hi mom!"

"Are you okay?"

She asks, sounding deeply concerned because the truth is, I've not called or gone by her house in a while. I genuinely plan to but stuff always pop up and I don't bother. Now that I am able to embrace a better perspective, I admit that for years I have resented her. I've resented her for not protecting me more, for not protecting us. I hated her for what I perceived as weakness but now I realize that it took more strength and courage for her to stay than to leave. Now I'm able to see that she stayed for me, her child, more than anything else. Oh, the irony!

There is silence for a bit then invariably she says,

"How is Cyril? I didn't get a chance to speak with him at the funeral. He must be devastated! Poor baby!"

"He's fine mom! I just left his house! We had dinner tonight!"

"Oh, that's wonderful!"

She says, sounding excited about a dinner to which she hadn't been invited. I can see her clasping her hands as she says this. She always does that when she is excited.

"Mom, do you know someone by the name of Zimera? She's a friend of aunt Felecie?"

"No baby! That name doesn't sound familiar".

"Ok, just wondering".

"Sorry I couldn't help baby. But how do you know her?"

"I met her tonight at Cyril's and since she was a friend of auntie's I thought you knew her".

"Baby what exactly did she say about me?" She asks sounding a little strange.

"Nothing mom! I was just wondering since you and auntie were kinda close!"

"Anyways, mom I have to go. I was just checking in".

"Ok baby, thanks for checking in".

"Good night mom! I...I love you! Thank you for all you've done for me! I just want you to know that I so appreciate all you've done for me!"

I promptly hang up. I don't wait for her reaction, none is required. This is new territory for both of us. I have not said I love her in years. I always felt like a hypocrite saying it so when she did, I just didn't bother to respond. However, not tonight! Tonight, it genuinely feels good to say it.

I wonder briefly how Cyril is doing. He did not seem impressed with Zimera at all.

Chapter 20

Cyril's Dilemma

After they both leave, I am left shaking my head, like literally SMH. What is up with this lady? Where does she get the gall to spew so much bull in my house? It is ridiculous! She seems to have manipulated Austin into accepting her crap but not me!

Clearly, Zimera might be able to trick Austin into accepting this rubbish but not me. I'm stronger than that. I will not be deceived. Because you know what, I have built a world that I'm comfortable in. A world where I have always dictated the pace. Do you know why? Because, I have to feel in control. There have been many times when I felt like my life was spiralling out of control; especially, as a child. There were times when I felt really helpless and hopeless and I absolutely never wish to feel this way ever again.

For instance, on the day when I lost the love of my life. Let's see, how old would he be now, or her? Maybe like seven. Who would he be like? Would he be like me or Preet? Would Preet and I be happily married or miserable? I don't know but I really wish I had gotten a chance to find out. That's the problem, I'll never know! Regret is the most horrible thing in the world. This world can be so unkind and cruel. Why should I let my guard down, like ever? Every time I do, I pay dearly for it. How can I let go of all I know to be good and true? So many questions that I will never receive an answer to. Zimera has no clue how hard it is to be me. My struggles are real and my pain is valid. It is very expensive to be me!

I have been on my own for a really long time, but I've never missed my mom the way I do now. I feel so robbed not ever knowing who my mom is. Both my parents as a matter of fact. I have so many questions! Am I more like my mom or my dad? This is something very minute in the grand scheme of things; however, when a child grows up without mother or father, it is the little things that are most significant. Do I have her smile? Will my kids have her smile? But of course, I might never know. I might be passing her everyday and still wouldn't know her from a can of pain.

I try to forget about mom and the conversation at dinner. I can't sleep again. Zimera's absence still rests on me, much like her presence did. I try not to think about her discourse at dinner because I'm so exhausted. I don't need any help in staying awake. I am fully capable of doing that all by myself. Sleep evades me so I am left with my thoughts or her *prognosis*. That stupid word "forgiveness" blankets me and I find it difficult to repel.

When I'm disturbed by a word, a concept or a scenario; I often try to find a replacement or a substitute word, phrase or scenario. However, the only word stuck on repeat in my head is *Zimera*. Because when you have spent your whole life creating your armour, anything that seeks to intrude is met with very hostile resistance. This armour becomes your second skin, a second home.

I cannot shake the feeling that Zimera is still with me and will be with me for a while, not in a physical way, but in a, what's the word, like a spiritual connection. Well, it must be extreme exhaustion because despite my efforts or in-spite of, I start to create a mental list of the things I need to forgive myself for. Obviously, some-things are easier to rehash than others so I stick with the easy stuff. Baby steps! This exercise is strangely calming and in about twenty minutes, I feel the hands of sleep ushering me away. It is like my reward for starting the process. This I don't resist. I just let sleep take me away in her gentle arms.

Chapter 21

Austin's Transformation

    I've never been a person who ever wanted to or saw a need to change my paradigm. But lately, I've been really examining myself, my very existence. I guess I've been having an existential crisis this whole time, without giving into it.

    It has been almost two months since the dinner at Cyril when I met Zimera but it seems like just yesterday. A lot has happened since then but mostly good things. The most significant, is the fact that mom and I have reconciled; in the sense that, I call her more, instead of ignoring her calls and I've gone to her house for dinner several times. There was that one time when Cyril came and he seemed to have left in better spirits; especially, since mom made all his favourites. Mostly, I'm ok with that because we like basically the same things; however, I do wish she would stop trying to mother him. Cyril is fine. He doesn't need a mom. He has been on his own for a long time. What he needs is a wife. I am not jealous or anything, but whenever he's around mom seems to pay him all the attention. I guess she must be star struck; plus, he's really handsome and charming – when he wants to be. I try not to dwell on that too much because I do feel fortunate that I have her and I've had her all my life; while, Cyril has lost everyone he loves. I suddenly feel guilty for being jealous.

Again, one of the changes I am committed to making in my life: to not look at what other's have but to count my blessings, daily. Also, not to dwell on the negatives around me, to make life happen instead of being a victim of life. Let's face it man, bad things happen to everyone, it's just part and parcel of the human experience. No one escapes this world unscathed eh! Therefore, it's just best to learn the lessons that life is teaching so we can move on. Clearly, every time I have failed a test in life, I have had to resist that exam. I am not about going backwards, forward is my end game. I feel so good about my life now: I have started to enjoy my job more and I am not even bothered by traffic anymore. I just listen to music or Cyril's stand up routine. Dude is a genius. I now intentionally give a place of prominence to the positives in my life instead of being angry at the negatives. I endeavour to approach each day with an intensity that if I died, I would be ok with death. Perspective is really a game changer.

Be that as it may, the greatest change is that I've started dating again. I have been meeting some really interesting women and while I am not actually thinking about marriage: I am definitely not as opposed to it as I once was. Previously, I was so anti-marriage that at the very idea of marriage my reaction was almost always a visceral one – a violent shudder.

I have even been trying to bring Cyril on a double date but that's a no go. I thought I was anti-marriage but dude is anti-relationships as well. Why do I always measure my happiness against his? I guess that's what friends are for. Come to think of it, I've been calling Cyril all day and he hasn't responded yet. I even texted him a few times. I wonder if he's out of town for a gig? But usually he tells me when he's going to be away. Oh well, I guess I'll just go by his house and chill for a few hours before my date this evening.

Chapter 22

Cyril's Crisis

Austin

There's a Jamaican proverb that my mom and her friends often quote: *trouble nuh set up like rain* (it is impossible to predict when there will be a crisis in your life; therefore, you can not be prepared for it). This is exactly what I walked into today.

After I had been calling and texting Cyril for a while without any response, I decide to go by his nest. I get to his house and his car is in the driveway so I knew he was home. I breathed a sigh of relieve but that was short lived. I walk through the house, yelling his name but there is still no response.

Eventually, I find him on the floor of his bathroom, on his back with foam and blood oozing from his mouth. Instantly, I realize that he has had a seizure. He had seizures as a kid but he has not had an episode since high school. We all thought he had been healed but possibly all the stress of the past few months triggered it again.

I was yet to become aware of the severity of the situation.

I call 911 and the paramedics are there in less than fifteen minutes and within the hour Cyril is being prepped for emergency surgery. Apparently, maybe from he was a kid, he has had a brain tumour which has been *exalted* (this is the word the doctors keep using) by the recent stress he's endured. The frequent headaches were his body's way of crying out for help and despite his many promises, "to look into it" he never even made an appointment to see a doctor. I doubt he even has a personal physician. Who could blame the guy, look what a physician did to his girlfriend?

He is currently in need of blood urgently because apparently his brain was bleeding for a while.

It turns out that I am a perfect match. According, to the attending doctors this is awesome because this saves time in sourcing the right blood type. They say, in this case what he needs most is the "platelets" because his blood needs to clot as clotting is the body's natural defence mechanism. Clotting is a concern because if after the surgery they can't get his blood to clot then he might die. I do not think about Cyril dying. I cannot. How would I live? Mom would be devastated as well to lose auntie and Cyril in the space of a few months. It would be too much to bear.

I am currently on autopilot, some of the day's events are a blur. How can I live in a world where my friend is absent? I call mom and she said that she is on her way. Thankfully, Cyril will never be alone in the world because he has us. Through tears I think I hear her say,

"My son!" In reference to Cyril but I think the shock of the moment has confused her. She also says, "It's time for you boys to hear the truth, once and for all!"

The truth? What truth? Mom is really losing it. The one time I need her to be strong!

Chapter 23

The Big Reveal

Austin

I hover in the waiting room with other families. Families with small children who are fussing – distracting their parents from their worry, others with older, more mature family members. We all have that same disheveled, far a way expression in our eyes, as if somehow, we're all trapped in the same nightmare, privy to the same horrific images.

I move to get a coffee, on my way to the elevator I see mom. In all the years of Stacy's abuse, I have never seen her look this way before: tears, snot, the whole works. Not quiet tears either but loud, obnoxious sobbing and a torrential downpour. I manage to calm her for a moment and explain to her that the surgery will last for at least five more hours so in the meanwhile we should go to the cafeteria downstairs. She pulls herself together and just when I thought I had heard everything, she rocks my world.

She quietly says, "Cyril is my son, your older brother!"
SHIT! I am beyond shocked.

This is my mom's tale. She says, between sobs:

I had Cyril when I was really, really young and I really couldn't take care of him. His dad Vince was a few years older but he was such a *mama's boy* he refused to share the responsibility of taking care of his son. On top of that, his mother was a piece of work. No one would ever be good enough for her prized son. From day one, his mom never accepted me. She said the meanest things to me when she saw me in the streets. Plus, Vince was never the type to stand up to his mom. I felt like I was fighting a losing battle. The family didn't mind Cyril as much because he looks so much like his dad but there was just no place for me in their world. I knew that it would have been an uphill battle; especially, with Cyril's mom. All that drama would have been too much for me. It was a very, very tough and painful choice but I knew that I would be an outcast in that family.

On the other hand, there was aunt Felecie. She knew too well her mother's wrath so she was always sympathetic towards me. She was the only member of Vince's family who would stop by to check on me and baby Cyril and she always brought a gift. It became too overwhelming to be a mom. On top of that, my mom was angry with me for "throwing away yu life by having a pickney (child) too soon". She often, threatened to throw me and Cyril out of her house because at her age, she did not want to hear any crying at night. Where would we go? It was just me and Cyril against the world.

I could fight and I did fight, but how could I win? The magnitude of my situation became too crushing. I had to make a choice, not only for me, but for my child as well.

One day, I found myself walking towards Vince's house and before I knew it, I had placed Cyril in aunt Felecie's strong, capable arms and was walking away. I did not dare look back, for fear that my resolve would have been shaken. With tears rolling down my face and a deep sense of loss and guilt, I left my baby boy behind – my only child behind. I left him to a fate and a future that was unknown. How could I leave him behind? What choice did I have really? The sad part is that afterwards, no one in my family ever asked about Cyril; it was as if he never even existed. It was almost as if I hadn't given birth to a living, breathing human being. They might have forgotten but I never did. By that time, I had gone to Secretarial school, one of the few options available to me at the time in rural Jamaica.

A year or so later, still deeply broken and reeling from my loss, I met Stacy and we fell in love. He was handsome, intelligent and charming. He was teaching at the time.

Did you know your dad had been a teacher back home? I said I didn't and she continued.

When I brought him home, it was like he had somehow made up for my having a baby, my mistake. My family worshipped Stacy and they constantly reminded me that I was lucky to have him - not the other way around. After a brief courtship, we got married. It was shortly after that I discovered that aunt Felecie had emigrated to Canada with Cyril. Being from a small community, going to any foreign country was a huge deal and that type of news travelled fast.

Armed with that knowledge, I did everything in my power to convince Stacy to move to Canada; to be near to my baby. At the time, I had absolutely no idea where in Canada aunt Felecie had moved to. But as fate would have it, Felecie moved to Brampton after Vince died and lived so close to us, it was a miracle. It was as if I had been given a second chance and I wasn't about to mess it up! Not this time. Up to that point, I had not told Stacy about my son: my mom had warned against it. What if he left me? Just let sleeping dogs lie my mom said. So, I never told Stacy, even after I discovered that Cyril was attending the same school where I worked. It was a dream come true; far more than I deserved, so I couldn't risk it. Plus, by then Stacy had changed so dramatically that I was terrified for both my sons. Can you imagine the turmoil if Stacy had even stumbled upon this truth, after being married for so many years? It was far too unbearable to consider.

On top of that, Stacy was already enraged with me for "making" him leave his *"good, good job and come a Canada fe suffer and live beneat me pay grade"*. He was beyond angry that he could not get a job in his field. He would have had to go back to school. An expense we couldn't afford. By then we had, had you Austin and things were extremely tight – not at all what any of us had anticipated. So, disappointment after disappointment, left a wound in your dad's soul; a wound so all consuming that only God and time can heal. And you mustn't be angry with him Austin, because it is a part of the human condition to get hung up on what was supposed to be as opposed to what is. Stacy is not the first human to fall victim to the disillusionment of the Canadian dream. A dream that is so obscure that not many immigrants find it. Some even give up and return to their country of origin. But I could not leave my baby, not again. The last time almost killed me.

Later, I had heard from some teachers at school that if we moved out West, a bit more snow and quite cold, but life might be easier. Vince might be able to find a teaching job out there. The problem was, how would I convince Felecie to move with us? She had already had her world turned upside down one too many times and I could not risk her cutting off all contact with me – so I just couldn't pressure her. It would not be fair. She also had her personal demons fighting with and at least I was near enough to assist with Cyril, if push came to shove, which sometimes happened. I was just a phone call away.

In the end, I know I was being extremely selfish and unfair to Stacy but I had to choose my child: flesh of my flesh and bone of my bone. You do understand that, don't you baby?

Despite the growing body of evidence, I refused to accept that Stacy was so badly broken. After all, he is a man so I thought that his bounce back game was stronger. How could I have predicted that one decision would have robbed him of his soul? And you know what, truth be told, I would do it all again in a heartbeat. I would still choose my child again and again. In this life Austin, sometimes we are called upon to make unimaginable sacrifices, ones that no human should be called upon to make. But of such is the cycle of life, here on planet Earth.

Both Felecie and I decided to keep our secret and helped each other as much as we could. Finally, I got to spend time with both my sons; so much so that, an even bigger dream was fulfilled: you both became friends with little to no prodding. Indeed, every mother's dream.

So, there you have it my son, my truth and I just hope both you and Cyril can forgive me for the deception and the betrayal.

Austin

Wow! Just wow! My head is spinning. To think all of that had been orchestrated by both my mom and aunt Felecie who died with her secret. Because I'm pretty sure, Cyril – my brother – knows nothing about this. Looking back, all of this makes perfect sense. For starters, my mom being a secretary at a school and deciding to take home someone's kid; that's unheard of in Canada. This is not Jamaica where rules are amendable, or just made up as you go along. That was extremely dangerous, the police could have gotten involved. Also, that time when aunt Felecie had lost it and locked Cyril in her apartment, it was my mom who had gone there to check on them and called the police when my aunt refused to open the door. It was mom who volunteered to keep him for a while so that he wasn't placed in the foster care system. I don't even know how she had managed to pull that one off. Plus, all the albums with pictures of Cyril, she had given them to aunt Felecie.

In that moment, it all came together for me.

Talk about the big reveal: my head is spinning!

Chapter 24

Fiona's Relief

I am so happy I finally got to share all this with Austin. I am really hoping I'll be able to share it with my son Cyril as well. I didn't know that I'd be sharing this tale at a time like this in a hospital cafeteria. The last time when they both came over for dinner I had built up the courage to tell them. I even asked my husband to go out for the night. But, Cyril still seemed so sad, he was still in mourning. I mean, he was charming and engaged; after all, he is Vince's son, but I could still see the signs of sadness in him: a mother instinctively knows these things. I did not want to drop this on him. I didn't want to run the risk and lose him forever. I couldn't take that chance. I figured that I had been patient for so many years, a few months or even a few more years would not make any difference. And right there is one of the fundamental problems plaquing humanity: we always think we have time, lots of time, until we don't have anymore time.

Also, the fact that Austin was talking to me again: the fact that he wanted me in his life, meant that I would also have Cyril in my life. From the first day they met, they've been a team until now. I cannot even begin to imagine how many secrets they share between them. After so many years, I finally got my son back, both of them and now this.

Cyril is still in surgery and a nurse came to inform us that so far, the surgery was going well; however, if there were still signs of bleeding after this surgery, they would have to put him in a coma. Can you imagine that? I feel like I'm just coming out of a coma myself, I feel like I'm just able to breathe again and now this!

I visit the chapel that is next door to the hospital and say a prayer, while hot tears wash my face. I pray for Austin as well. I pray for his strength; after all, to just discover that he has a brother and to lose him all on the same day and the same place would be unbearable. I feel like I would lose both my children and my mind if that were to happen.

This must be my punishment and if it is I'll gladly accept it but please God, don't punish my children for my mistakes. Maybe, if I had been more attentive to Cyril. Maybe, if I had forced Felecie to take him to a specialist when he was little. I don't mean to sound ungrateful and judgmental towards Felecie, because she was a mother to him when I couldn't be and in all her struggles with mental health and family issues, she did right by my Cyril. She always put him first even when I couldn't. So, I don't mean to criticize her but I just wish that I had given more to Cyril, I just wish I had been enough for both my children.

I'm so sorry I had married a man named Stacy. Maybe if I had made a better choice in a life partner I could have told Cyril years ago. Maybe if I had not been living in fear all those years, I could have stepped up to the plate. I don't know. I've made a point of not living in regret, but today that's all I feel; regret.

Austin, comes to get me: wonderful, sturdy, reliable Austin. He takes one look at me and says,

"Mom, have you been crying all this time?"

"You cannot blame yourself for this mom!"

"Why not?"

"I'm his mom, I should have been more attentive! After all, he is my child, my responsibility! I should have gotten rid of Stacy earlier, but if I did, he would not have helped you through university! I absolutely had to stay for your sake baby! I had a choice to make. I had all these horrible choices to make but I should not have been so afraid!"

"No mom! You did the best you could under less than perfect conditions! You should not blame yourself! Cyril is an adult; he should have paid closer attention to his health! You can not be a superhero to everyone, ok! I love you and I'm pretty sure Cyril will be fine and he *will* forgive you as well. Don't forget that we were both witnesses to Stacy's bad temper".

"Thank you, Baby. But a mother is supposed to protect her children at all cost!"

"Mom, you said it yourself, Stacy would not have

helped. What would have been the point to destroy so many lives? Also, what would have happened to aunt Felecie if you had taken Cyril? Cyril was her whole world; it would not have been fair".

"I guess you're right my son!"

"In life, we all have to make choices using the information that's available to us. Now if you make choices from the purity of your heart, with whatever info you have, you cannot blame yourself when things happen in the future!"

"You're right!"

"You can not punish yourself forever! You can not live with regret forever. I know this for a fact that it will eat away at you, little by little, and before you know it, it erodes your soul. Do not do this to yourself. This is exactly what Cyril wouldn't have wanted you to do".

"I know, but it's hard!"

"I know it's hard but it is not impossible! A few months ago, I met a lady, Zimera…"

"The lady you were asking about? I thought she had shared my secret with you. I was terrified!"

"I realize that now. No, she taught me the power of forgiveness. She taught me that, if I continue to hold on to regret, then it turns into self hate and eventually it would destroy my soul because then I would merely be existing and not truly living! She was and still is a stranger to me, but I took her advice and today I'm a better man, a better son, a better friend, a better brother because of it!"

I sigh and hug my son, my baby. When did he become

so smart? He definitely has an old soul!

He places his hands on my shoulder and looks me dead in the eye and says,

"Promise me, that whatever happens from here on; whether Cyril makes it or not, that you will not punish yourself. That you will learn to live again".

I said I would and I meant it, even for him. Because he too has suffered as a result of my choices so don't I at least owe him that? He said,

"As a matter of fact, where is your husband? Shouldn't he be here with you?"

I tell him that I haven't told my new husband any of this because I'm too ashamed. Plus, our relationship has been strained over the last few months, ever since Felecie died.

He says, "Mom, you got a second chance at happiness. Please do not allow guilt to create a wedge in your marriage. After everything that you've been through, if anyone deserves to be happy, you deserve it. You've had to make hard choices, choices that a mom should not be called upon to make but you did and you survived".

"We all have to make choices son".

"Yes, we do! But sometimes life just puts our back up against the wall and in that moment, we have a choice: sink or swim. You swam mom and because you chose to swim, I'm able to swim. Cyril is a fighter of this I'm sure. So, in my heart, I know he's going to be fine. And if it happens that he doesn't make it, there's a greater purpose at stake here".

I flinch when he says this. Why should I be called

upon to make more sacrifices? Why should I sacrifice anything else in this world?

"I am not saying he's going to die mom. I'm just saying that sometimes we don't have control over what happens so we just have to do the best we can and accept whatever decision that fate hands us".

I close my eyes, to stop the tears. He hugs me so tightly, as if he's trying to squeeze faith back into me. How can I let him down? How I can I fail him again?

"Ok baby, I will choose to be strong, not only for you and Cyril but for myself as well".

"That's my girl! Let's go and see if there's any new developments with Cyril!"

"Ok son, we can do this!" I exclaim with a conviction that I don't feel.

"Yes, we can mom!"

Chapter 25

Cyril's Miracle

On the fateful morning of my surgery, I woke up with a severe headache. I had grown accustomed to going to sleep with a headache and waking up with a headache. This headache was different: it was one of those pounding headaches that felt like there was a little man in my head with a huge jack hammer. I had been planning for weeks to see my personal physician but I hate doctors so it was a matter of building up the courage to see her. I'm assuming that I went to shower and I passed out – because that's where Austin said he had found me – good old, reliable Austin. I owe him my life and that's one debt I can not repay.

But imagine me, coming out of surgery and finding aunt Fiona in tears. I was deeply touched by her tears. Early, the following morning she was still there, wearing the same clothes from the previous day. She then said that she had asked the doctors' permission to share something with me. I remember that I was still groggy, but I asked her, "Auntie why would you ever need anyone's permission to speak with me?"

She said, "Son" ……That's exactly how she addressed me, with tears in her eyes.

"Son, what I have to tell you is very important and might be difficult for you to hear".

I said, "OK", caught between, both wanting to hear and *not* wanting to hear. For all I knew, she was about to tell me that Austin had died or worse, that Zimera had returned. That lady is incorrigible man – yes, that's the word I've been searching for all this time. I have fully had enough of her bull.

She then proclaimed four words which reoriented my life forever, gave me peace and addressed some of my hardest questions. Four simple words which have changed the trajectory of my life for the better.

She solemnly declared, "I am your mother".

SHIT!

I hollered and bawled so loudly that nurses came flying from every direction. But they soon discerned from all the hugging that they were tears of joy. Austin was there too as usual. He cried more than I did.

After all these years, life is so funny man, you never know what's going to happen from one moment to the next. Can you imagine waking out of a coma and being hit with that kind of news? It's insane, I'm not gonna lie though, it is good news; it is fabtastic news (my new word that I created just for this situation). I haven't had much of those in a while so I'll take it. As shocked as I was, well, I guess the meds helped to cushion the blow, I guess deep down, I had always seen Austin and his mom, no our mom, as family. Another one of my aunt's favourite sayings and chief among them was, *wha nuh happen in a year, happen in a day*. It took me a while to grasp the meaning but today I do. This could not be truer of my situation.

What am I saying though? The signs were always there but I was too distracted to pay attention. From the very first day that we met, I was young but I remember feeling an instant connection to her. I felt connected to both Austin and auntie.... I mean mom. But not Stacy though. He is clearly not my tribe. Now that I think about it, mom has done more than hover on the periphery of my life. She has been there for all my important moments, all my milestones. In fact, it was her who bought me my very first bike and threw my first and only birthday party. Looking back, she has always had a soft spot for me. She has always had my best interest at heart. Mom had even offered to pay my university tuition but that was not an offer I could have accepted because I knew she was struggling as well.

The fact is, I have spent so much of my adult life worrying and obsessing about Preet, that I could not see the things that really mattered most: my family – auntie, mom, and Austin. If I weren't so distracted all the time, they might have told me sooner – but I was always in a hurry to get away from them. Who knows? I can only focus on what is before me right now. They have always been ubiquitous to my existence. I am finally persuaded to allow that painful part of my life, my Preet Saga, to die a natural death.

It has been exactly six months since my surgery and since then I've had: rehab, physiotherapy, and more physiotherapy. Also, after the initial surgery they had to put me in a coma because there was still some bleeding on my brain. I think in total they've done three surgeries. I'm just glad to be a live and I am healing slowly, but slow and steady wins the race. I don't expect a fairytale ending, that is just not real and while that might be another person's experience, it has most certainly not been mine. So, I'm prepared to spend the time and do whatever it takes to heal. I hear lots of people on social media talking about "self love" which seems ironic to me. When did that become a thing? Isn't it a given that we love ourselves? I guess not!

I fought so hard to resist what Zimera was saying but only to discover now that she was right all along. I have to forgive myself. I have to give myself permission to grieve and to move on. I've been stuck at one spot for a number of years, I sometimes feel like I was going around in circles: sleep, stress, eat, perform, repeat. I'm not living that way anymore. Don't I have a right to be healthy, to be whole? Why should I devote my life to heal others through laughter but remain broken? Hell, to the no! From now on, I'm putting myself first! Cyril comes first!

I actually had a dream about Zimera a few weeks ago – again – because I am just now remembering that early spring I had a dream where I had heard her name. At the time, I didn't know this, but it was like a pronouncement of her arrival. Also, I guess because of the tumour and the headaches I could not remember the dream at the time or maybe I just wasn't supposed to remember it. That was definitely for the best. It would have been weird to dream about her and voila, she appeared. That would have been scary.

I also remember the dead boy in my dream. At first, I thought he was my dead son, the one that I had killed, but then I realize that, that boy is me. I had died a slow and painful emotional death. Zimera made an appearance at a very crucial point in my life to heal me from the wounds that had been inflicted in my soul. Now, the horrible memories no longer haunt me. I am learning to accept the things that I cannot change. And yes, to forgive myself for the choices I've made. After all, aren't we all allowed to make mistakes? Isn't that part and parcel of the human experience? You best believe I'm going to sleep better now, knowing that from time to time I will mess up and while I do have to hold myself accountable, I'm not going to be that hard on myself ever again.

In addition, to seeing a physiotherapist, I've been seeing a psychologist, who is helping me to put things in perspective. Another one of Zimera's words. That's going great! This doesn't mean that it's easy to unearth and disturb all the memories I've buried. But like physical healing, that too is a very slow process; however, I'm willing to put in the time, because I'm worth it.

Fortunately, for me, I don't harbour any fantasies anymore; therefore, I no longer have any preconceived notion of how things should be. I've decided to live in the present and enjoy every moment. I've spent a lot of years tied to the past, reliving past hurts and disappointments. However, thanks to the surgery, I now have a new lease on life. My life is far from perfect, as I still have a lot of unlearning and learning to do.

My psychologist, Dr Savannah Parish, actually told me that it is way more difficult to unlearn something than to learn it in the first place. Dr Parish said I should start journaling as this will help with dealing with my issues. Who knew writing could be so therapeutic. However, sometime it is painful to read the events that I've described on paper but it becomes easier to frame a situation once I see it in black and white. Also, like I told her, I'm willing to put in the work and fight for my life. I didn't just get this way overnight and I do not want to rush the process either. I have good days and bad days. Also, she thinks that my family and I should plan a trip to Jamaica because sometimes visiting our ancestral home is healing as it grounds our very existence in the world. I definitely will as soon as I get a chance to.

Sometimes, it is eerie how much of what Zimera had said that night has been echoed by Dr Savannah. Back then, I really wasn't ready to hear the harsh truths but I am ready now. That word forgiveness is so powerful. Through my doctor's help I've come to recognize that I also needed to forgive aunt Felecie as well, for abandoning me and for the abuse during my childhood. She reminded me that aunt Felecie did what she could with the skills that she had learned from her own mom.

That's all she was doing, regurgitating what she knew. Also, that not forgiving others would leave me in a cycle of repeating past mistakes and stuck in a pattern, reliving the same life over and over again. My one regret is that, I did not have the mindset that I now have in order to help aunt Felecie. Maybe, if I had insisted on therapy, then she would be hear now. She would have experienced her own rebirth. Who knows? Of necessity, I'm going to have to forgive myself for abandoning my auntie during a critical period in her life as well.

Days, often spent disrupting old patterns of thinking – those days leave me weak and vulnerable – without my shield. Thankfully, on those days I can speak with mom. She is quite similar to Zimera in a way that I've never allowed myself to see before. Mom is quiet, gentle and soothing. Her welcome presence has an extremely calming effect.

I have definitely discovered more about myself. I have discovered that I've loved a lot of things and a lot of people but I've never truly loved myself; flaws and all. That's going to change real quick because after a show and the crowd leaves, I'm left with myself. I am always going to go home with myself so why not learn to appreciate the skin am in.

Also, I've discovered that am not unique in anyway and that lots of other people are locked in a world of pain. Therefore, I've made the decision that moving forward, my comedy is going to have an added dimension. A dimension that will call out our human failings and call out our inability to seek to heal properly. I'll be calling out the BS that we surround ourselves with, which blocks our growth. Yes, for sure, things are going to be different. I certainly didn't come this far, just to come this far.

Life is grand and I am here for all of it; the good and the bad.

Chapter 26

Cyril's Show

It has been exactly ten months since my surgery and with the support of my family, I have experienced a rebirth. I am also in talks with a publisher to write a book, chronicling my struggles with depression. I know some will be skeptical about yet another celebrity writing a book and that's fine, because my purpose is bigger; hence, my decision clearer. I believe that being a part of the human race demands that, after we have come to a crossroad in our journey and learned a critical lesson, it becomes imperative that we pass on the lesson to the rest of humanity. Who knows, you might be saving a life! Also, I'm not gonna lie, a movie might be in the works as well. This movie would not just be about me though. It would be a look at the life and times of my auntie, eulogizing her in high definition, for all the world to see because without her, there would be no Cyril Parks.

Tonight, is my first show in a while and I am ready, every vein, all my nerve endings: I'm just raring to go. My fans have really been great as well. Imagine, having such a huge support system and being unaware of it. Imagine being loved by so many and not allowing myself time to notice.

Love is an extremely powerful magic and if people only know that they are loved and wanted – valued; they will soar. Being chosen is a powerful thing which comes with a responsibility to also choose: choose to live, choose to love; instead of, always leaving it up to people to choose you.

I have acknowledged that I have to learn to not only give but to receive love as well. So much to learn and unlearn but I'm here for it.

Tonight, I perform to a sold-out crowd in Toronto. My fans applaud for a good fifteen minutes before I am allowed to begin. For the first time since I have been performing, I invite my family to come on stage and I introduce them by saying, "if you ever see these humans misbehaving, just know that they belong to me". Again, a roar of applause at my cheesy humour. I tell them about my brother and his ferocious loyalty, my mom's big heart, even my step father is introduced. I don't really know him that well yet, but there is still time. My audience applauds boisterously for another ten minutes. I also tell them a little about my aunt Felecie who raised me and through her love and guidance I am the man that I am. I also mention Zimera.

I know this is farfetched, but I actually sense Zimera's presence sometimes. Isn't that funny! I went from resenting her to some how graving her presence. I am a changed man my friends! Anyways, I hope that where ever she is, that she is well.

Finally, I am no longer angry at or ashamed of where my lineage comes from or confused about my origin. I realize that after all these years, I've been ashamed of my family, ashamed of my roots ashamed of myself; but not anymore.

As the song by the famous Jamaican Jimmy Cliff says:

> I can see clearly now the rain is gone
> I can see all obstacles in my way
> Gone are the dark clouds that had me blind
> It's gonna be a bright (bright)
> Bright (bright) sunshiny day
> It's gonna be a bright (bright)
> Bright (bright) sunshiny day.

Which for me in no way asserts that life will be perfect, but that life will be lived on a grander scale, now that the scales have fallen from my eyes and I am deliberately choosing to be grateful every single day. I think that's what aunt Felecie would have wanted – that is what she was describing in our last conversation – and doing so will honour her memory.

Epilogue
Zimera

In my spirit form, I have stopped by to check on the boys. Cyril is working hard on his healing. Austin is pretty much whole again. Fiona has managed to forgive herself and her marriage has flourished. They have all discovered that all their imperfections make them uniquely perfect and they have decided to choose themselves every single day.

They now realize that they have made mistakes and they will continue to make mistakes but the important thing is to deal with each mistake on its own merit; instead of trying to lump them all together and then end up with a pile up of emotions. Emotions are already tricky things so lumping all their emotions together is definitely not healthy.

I am actually pleased with myself. My work here is done. I will check in on them occasionally but I think they got this and they will be fine! They now know that they have each other and that's one of the greatest lessons us ancestral spirits like to impart: the love of the family.

Mission accomplished!
Now to go visit another family somewhere else.

Acknowledgements

Zimera is the first book I ever wrote. I wrote it at a time when I was battling a case of chronic sciatica and I wrote to ward of the depression threatening to overwhelm me. This, my baby, has been long in coming and now that she is here I am eternally grateful to all the people who have encouraged me in one way or the next. They are quite literally too numerous to mention, but you know yourselves so take a bow. To all the people who have inspired me keep on shining; sometimes the rest of us need your light to find our way. Thank you John "Toby" Cadham and Barbara Stewart Edwards for taking time out of your extremely busy schedule to help me with the editing process; much appreciated, your input was necessary. Toby, thank you for having my back; you are indeed a gift to humanity.

To all my loved ones who have transitioned, I cherish every memory we've made and I carry you in my heart everyday.

Last but by no means least, thanks be to God for being my all in all; never would have made it without You. It is Your favour that sustains me from day to day. It is You who dream dreams for me and give me vision.

Do not go gentle into that good night
Dylan Thomas - 1914-1953

Do not go gentle into that good night,
Old age should burn and rave at close of day;
Rage, rage against the dying of the light.

Though wise men at their end know dark is right,
Because their words had forked no lightning they
Do not go gentle into that good night.

Good men, the last wave by, crying how bright
Their frail deeds might have danced in a green bay,
Rage, rage against the dying of the light.

Wild men who caught and sang the sun in flight,
And learn, too late, they grieved it on its way,
Do not go gentle into that good night.

Grave men, near death, who see with blinding sight
Blind eyes could blaze like meteors and be gay,
Rage, rage against the dying of the light.

And you, my father, there on the sad height,
Curse, bless, me now with your fierce tears, I pray.
Do not go gentle into that good night.
Rage, rage against the dying of the light.
From *The Poems of Dylan Thomas*, published by New Directions.

ABOUT THE AUTHOR

Kareen Lopez Samuels hails from the small island of Jamaica, a teacher of English by profession and she has been an educator for over twenty years. The first child and only girl for her parents – Winston Lopez and Beatrice Stone Lopez (now deceased). She attended the Osborne Store Primary School, then Glenmuir High School. After graduating high school, she attended the Mico College; now Mico University College in Kingston, Jamaica. She taught at Vere Technical High School for two years, then completed a Bachelor's Degree in Linguistics at the University of the West Indies, Mona, campus. Kareen later married Desmond Samuels and migrated to Ontario, Canada, where they currently live with their two girls: Abigail and Rachel. She also completed a Masters' degree in Language, Culture and Education at York University, the Keele Campus and an Honours Specialist in English from the same institution. She is currently employed to the Peel District School Board. She has always had an interest in writing and has written short stories, non-fiction, a few short plays and directed them at her local assembly.

For feedback, comments, etc., please contact Kareen at one of the following:
Email: kareensamuels@yahoo.com
Facebook: Kareen Lopez Samuels
Instagram: @toishma
Twitter: @toishma

AVAILABLE NOW
THEY WERE HERE BEFORE
"…We all carry, inside us, people who came before us."
Liam Callanan

Turn the page to read an extract from this insightful and revealing text.

Chapter 20
Nathan

I try to ward off sleep for as long as I can, like when I was a just a boy and I wanted to stay up late with my older cousins to hear stories about *Anansi,* the trickster figure, whose ingenuity always wins in the end. However, it is as if, I have had *Wild Dagga,* a plant well-known for its sleep-inducing property; I am way too exhausted to fight anymore. You know how sometimes, you gently slid into a peaceful sleep and slowly become aware of a dream; not me, not tonight. I am immediately pulled into a very harsh dream; Kacia and Shan are there as well. Once again, Kacia is under attack. I rush in, guns a blazed as the Americans would say, except there is no gun, ignoring the apparent danger to myself. I hear myself command, "Yeka lokhu!" *Stop this!* "Lokhu akusikho njengabantu!" *This is not us, as a people!* Why am I suddenly speaking Zulu, a language I hardly speak? Kacia's assailants immediately turn their attention to me like sunbathers facing Apollo.

At this point, I am operating purely on adrenaline and I can not even lie, I am scared beyond measure. I have never been this terrified in my whole life. It is not just the people and their strange clothing, or the sounds, or their grimacing and flailing, it is the place, it evokes a fear that is almost tangible; a fearful reverence. Intuitively, I know that this is a majestic place for the exalted, not a place for a weakling like me. Now that I have their attention, I fumble in my mind to find the most logical argument. As I am about to speak, something peculiar happens, as if on cue; they all bow their heads, an obeisance indicative of reverence. I am rendered speechless. Why are they doing this? Who are these people? Could they be my people? Instinctively, I know that I originated from them; that they were here before. But how are they here now? Why am I here now, in this place, at this time? What is the meaning of this?

Then after a silence that stretches for an eternity, so jarring, I feel it echo in my body, in my veins, like a delayed pulse; so much so, that I believe my heart would be silenced indefinitely: Shan takes charge of this extraordinary situation. Wonders never cease! Seemingly, she commands their attention like a true monarch. But as if that in itself is not confusing enough, what she says next sends shivers down my spine: "Lalela inkosann yakho!" *Listen to your prince!* Is Shan speaking Zulu? Why? How? What the *Mka* is going on here?

Immediately, I turn around - relief flooding me - to see this prince who has made an appearance, because I really would like to have a word with him. Plus, someone needs to take charge here and reveal to me (very slowly) what in the fuck is going on here. But alas, to my great and utter chagrin, no one is standing there; just me. Just me, in my mind I see myself clearly, a small boy, where a man should be. Is this how I have always seen myself – a mere effigy - of whom I am meant to be? Shan moves closer to me and instructs me like a trusted advisor, "Tell them to release the prisoner. I'll explain everything later!"

I am light headed! Is this going to be my permanent state from now on; light headedness? Because that is all I have been feeling all afternoon; light headed. I have experienced all the symptoms of a full-blown panic attack; however, the most terrifying is still looming -hyperventilation. Despite that and maybe because of that; the significance of the moment is not lost on me, as I am suddenly and painfully aware that Kacia's life greatly depends on everything I do, say, my tone and even my body language from here on. With a quiver in my voice, which I am useless to conceal, I command *my* people – who else could they be – I command them to "Muyeke ahambe!" *Let her go!* This command is met with immediate and vehement protest. I am no prince and that much is clear. However, I still have to try, so I raise my hand in a resolute stance and I search deep within for a harsh reprimanding glare. I guess it works. They reluctantly release Kacia. She is shaking from exhaustion and fear. Shan rushes to soothe, her lips moving quietly.

Surprisingly, I am awake, alive but quite unwell and back in Toishma's hut again – my stomach doing flips, drenched in sweat. Thankfully, it wasn't any other bodily fluids. What in thunderation is going on here? I make a silent vow to myself, from now on, I am never going back to sleep, not today, not tomorrow, not next month, not ever.

www.ingramcontent.com/pod-product-compliance
Lightning Source LLC
LaVergne TN
LVHW021720060526
838200LV00050B/2771